To Ladye Bay

by

Stephen Selby

To Kate,

Hope you enjoy the book. Keep swimming!

Steve xxx

Copyright © 2023 Stephen Selby

All rights reserved, including the right to reproduce this book, or portions thereof in any form. No part of this text may be reproduced, transmitted, downloaded, decompiled, reverse engineered, or stored, in any form or introduced into any information storage and retrieval system, in any form or by any means, whether electronic or mechanical without the express written permission of the author.

The views expressed in this work are solely those of the author and do not necessarily reflect the views of the publisher, and the publisher hereby disclaims any responsibility for them.

Cover painting courtesy of Nancy Farmer

ISBN: 9798867128678

PublishNation
www.publishnation.co.uk

Other books by the author

Sunrise

Instagram steveselbysteveselby

WE SWIM

We swim for salvation, we swim for our soul
We swim for the friendship, we swim to feel whole
We swim when it's raining, we swim in the snow
We swim in all weathers, wherever we go
We swim in the rivers, the lakes and the sea
We swim where we can, we swim to be free
We swim for adventure, we bounce with the waves
We jump from the rocks and we're pulled through the caves
We swim to raise spirits, we swim for release
We swim without judgement, we swim to find peace
We swim to remember, we swim to get by
We swim so we live, we will swim till we die.

Gertrude Higginbottom 1972

CONTENTS

Foreword

Introduction
Jeremy Won't Buy a Book

Page

PART ONE- CLEVEDON'S PAST

The First Clevedon Swimmers The Welsh Invaders	1
Jesus in Clevedon	5
Alfred the Great and the Vikings	8
Walton-Super-Mare	11
Gertrude's Childhood Birthday Gifts	14
The Invention of the Yo-yo Yo-yo	17
Gertrude's First Sea Swim	19
Betty and Mildred	21
The Monks' Steps	25
Gertrude and the Steps The Monks' Steps	27
Gertrude's First Ladye Bay Swim	28

A Mere Woman Kathleen	32
Perverts' Perch Perverts' Perch	36
Johnny Go Johnny	38
The Dryrobe Song	41
Gertrude's First Love	45
Clevedon Pier Oh, Clevedon Pier	47
Frederick Tebay- The People's Champion	52
Dogs in Clevedon	56
Betty the Record Breaker Mrs. Roberts	59
The Clevedon Mafia	63
The Monks' Trunks	68
Fins and Flippers Cheat Feet	70
The Clevedon 'Olympics'	73
Buckets and Spades	79
Pissy Corner Of Pissy Corner	82

Twenty-two Ways	86
A Sordid Tale	90
Swim From Suicide Rock From Suicide Rock	93
The War and Beyond War	98
Pilgrimage	102
Elvis in Clevedon	104
Stimulation's What You Need Stimulation's What You Need	108
Swimming With Her Majesty	111
Goodbye Gertie To Ladye Bay and Back	115
PART TWO- CLEVEDON'S PRESENT	119
Hail the Boring Bastards	120
The Swim and Tonics Song	122
Me and My Dryrobe	124
In the Bleak Midwinter	125
The Return of Naughty Sally Twinkle	128
The Boring Bastards Save the Day	132

The Curse of the Bossy Camper	**134**
Song of the Dawn Chorus	142
Near Death in the Graveyard	143
Little Swimmy Timmy	147
Tim	149
Five Years	150
Sidney and Senna	151
The Mermaid and the Poo	152
The Chocolate Boring Bastards	154
Professor Wolf	156
Me and My Cold Hands	157
The Tale of Stevie Wevie and his Cold Hands	**158**
Song of the Mermaids	166
Epilogue	**167**
Visit Clevedon	168

FOREWORD

My Granny Gertie loved to sit me down on her knee and tell me tales of the many swimming adventures she had in her youth. She brought that world alive to me, painting a vivid picture of life in Clevedon in the years before the Second World War. The stories of her friends Johnny and Freddie, the swimming friars, of Betty the dog and the days when the Clevedon swimming community was under the control of the mafia. Most of all, I loved hearing the stories of some of the epic swims she had in her youth. She told me about the day she became the first person to swim from Suicide Rock and come out of it alive. Then there was the story of her epic twenty-two-way Ladye Bay swim and, the one I loved the most, the story of how she became a world champion in front of her home crowd. I was there the day she swam with The Queen. but she always said that the world championship swim was her proudest moment.

Recently, we sadly lost my mother, Granny Gertie's only daughter, Isobel. I was fortunate enough to inherit many of my grandmother's swimming possessions. These included the gold medal which she won in those championships. I have the dryrobe and the tow float she received on her seventh birthday, which she wrote about so beautifully in her poem, 'Birthday Gifts'. I have her medals, trophies and certificates, old newspaper articles which she saved every time she made the news and many, many of her old swimming costumes, swim hats and goggles. These items will be put on display in the Clevedon town museum when I finally get round to sorting through them.

The best discovery from her belongings was her diary. I always knew she had kept a diary but I thought it was long gone. Working with the author of this book, we read through thousands of entries and chose the ones which we thought best told her story. We chose not to include the stories which earned her the nickname, 'Dirty Gertie'. Maybe those stories will see the light of day in the future.

I hope my grandmother's stories will come to life for you, in the same way that they did for me, when she sat me on her knee and told me them when I was a young child. She certainly had a wonderful and fascinating life and I am delighted that her memories will now be recorded in print.

Olivia Pattinson.

INTRODUCTION

Jeremy won't buy a book. I have spent the last few weeks carrying copies of my debut book, Sunrise, around. I have sold plenty. Of course, not everybody has bought one. I was hopeful that Jeremy would but, sadly, it was not to be. His rejection of my work hurt me badly and I was forced to write a poem about it to help me get over the loss.

Jeremy Won't Buy a Book

Jeremy won't buy a book
He says he's not that dim
Jeremy won't buy a book
He says my books too grim
He thinks my fans are out of touch
He says a tenner's way too much
Jeremy won't buy a book
He says it's not for him

Jeremy won't buy a book
He tells me with such glee
Jeremy won't buy a book
At least he won't from me
He's far too clever for my prose
When asked to pay, turns up his nose
Jeremy won't buy a book
He'll wait until it's free

Jeremy won't buy a book
He won't invade his stash
Jeremy won't buy a book
He says my book is trash
He'd rather pay to fix his bike
My poetry, he doesn't like

Jeremy won't buy a book
He won't part with his cash

Jeremy won't buy a book
He'll never join the queue
Jeremy won't buy a book
Looks down on those who do
Well, Jeremy can go without
It's Jezza's loss, I have no doubt
Jeremy won't buy a book
So, Jeremy, screw you.

    I accept, it isn't a very nice poem, especially the final line. I can only apologise for any hurt it caused to Jeremy. To atone, I set out to write a book which I hoped he would enjoy. Jeremy is a fully paid-up member of the Clevedon swimming community and I was sure he would love a book about the history of swimming in Clevedon.

    I spent many, many hours researching this book. I spent days in Clevedon library, scanning through old newspapers, looking for any snippets which could be included. I unearthed some fascinating stories but there were nowhere near enough to fill a book. Then, one day, I was contacted by an Olivia Pattinson. She had just inherited the diaries of her grandmother, Gertrude Higginbottom, after her mother and Gertie's only daughter, Isobel, had sadly passed away.

    All Clevedon swimmers know about Gertrude Higginbottom. Ask anyone at the lake and they will know that she swam the Ladye Bay swim with Her Majesty, Queen Elizabeth II. Gertie was a legend in the town in the 1920s and 30s and had some remarkable tales to share about the Clevedon swimming community before the war. She had made thousands of entries in her diary so, again, I had to spend many weeks and months reading through them all to find the entries most relevant to my book. I have only included a small number of her diary entries, but what I have included offers a fascinating insight into the Clevedon swimming community back in the day.

Thankfully, over the last few years, there has been a major revival of swimming in Clevedon. The restoration of the marine lake a few years ago means that people now travel to the lake from far and wide for a swim. This book is dedicated to all those who swim in the sea and lake at Clevedon, today and in the past. Hopefully, plenty of them will buy the book and be fascinated and entertained by the history of the place they know and love. Maybe, Jeremy will buy a copy. I won't be holding my breath though.

PART ONE

CLEVEDON'S PAST

THE FIRST CLEVEDON SWIMMERS

Gertrude Higginbottom wrote this wonderful piece about the first known swimmers in Clevedon. It was published in the much-missed Clevedon Telegraph in 1967.

I have been fortunate to have lived my entire life in Clevedon. I have been privileged to have been a part of the town's history and of a wonderful swimming community. There has been a swimming community in Clevedon for millennia and a walk around Clevedon will show signs everywhere of this glorious past.

It is believed that the Clevedon marine lake dates back to the early Iron Age. It was not originally built as a swimming facility. Instead, it was designed to capture fish on overtopping tides to provide a food source for the local community. Anybody who swims in the lake will know that the lake still captures fish to this day. The eels, crabs and fish were easy pickings for the locals once they had been trapped in the lake. There was no pier to fish from in those days so the design of the lake was revolutionary.

Unsurprisingly, the marine lake made the town a target for invaders from the south of Wales. The Welsh were very jealous of the lake as no such facility existed on the other side of the channel. The Welsh were keen sea swimmers and wanted somewhere to swim when the tide was out.

They were desperate to seize ownership of the lake. Boats had not yet been invented and the two Severn Bridges were yet to be built. A land trip from Penarth to Clevedon would have meant an incredibly long trip via Gloucester. It was, therefore, not a surprise when the decision was taken to invade Clevedon in the way they knew best- by swimming across the channel!

The Penarth to Clevedon swim is popular with serious swimmers in the present day, but it is seen as more of a leisure activity. In those days it was a matter of life and death. Even now, it is extremely dangerous and that is with boat support. Back then it was even more perilous and you have to admire the bravery of those invaders. They even had to swim without tow floats as their bright orange colour would have made them much more visible to those defending Clevedon from their attack. They were forced to negotiate the perilous shipping lanes whilst looking almost invisible to passing ships. Incredibly dangerous.

Still, the invaders kept coming and our lake was under constant threat. The strong currents meant that they did not always land in Clevedon. It was common for tides to be misjudged and for them to land in Weston-Super-Mare. The marine lake in Weston was not thought to be a target for the Welsh. Aside from being crap, there is no pontoon to jump from. The invaders may have been unaware they had landed in Weston and thought that they were fighting for the more prized Clevedon Lake. It seems likely that the Weston Lake was captured at some stage. A recent archaeological dig during a lake drain found the fossilised remains of a three thousand years old Welsh Cake, deep in the mud at the foot of the lake.

In order to defend the lake in Clevedon, a decision was taken to build the hillfort on Wain's Hill. The remains of the fort can still be seen today and it is a lovely place to visit and imagine the arrows being fired out to sea at invading Welsh swimmers. Without tow floats, the invaders would have been almost invisible until they got close to shore, so any shots fired would need to be accurate. Once they were under the cover of the cliffs, they would have been impossible to spot from atop Wain's Hill. Out of sight, they would have been able to swim up to the lake and emerge from behind the pump house, taking the Clevedonians by surprise, making the capture of the lake a formality. With no evidence that the lake was ever taken, it seems certain that many Welshmen would have lost their lives at sea over the years.

Eventually, the Welsh gave up on trying to capture the lake. Locals, however, were intrigued by the Welsh invaders efforts to swim across the channel. It wasn't long before people started dipping their toes into the lake and, within a few years, the lake had been taken over by swimmers. It is not known if the swimmers were able to coexist with the anglers.

I wrote this poem about this period in Clevedon's past in a school history lesson.

The Welsh Invaders

The Welsh invaders were after our lake
They crossed the channel, risking all in their swim
Without their tow floats, no chance for a break
They arrived cold and hungry, their futures looked grim
Then the arrows were fired, from the top of Wains Hill
And the Welsh they were dying, no time for goodwill
From the proud Clevedon folk, who felt no guilt
For the lake was theirs, it was they who had built

It in all of her glory, it was theirs to keep
So, swim back to Wales, to your valleys and sheep.

JESUS IN CLEVEDON

We all know the story of Jesus's trip to our shores as a youngster, which has been documented in the hymn, Jerusalem. He was brought to England by his uncle, Joseph of Arimathea, on a merchant voyage. His trip to Glastonbury is well known but how many are aware that he also visited Clevedon?

Jesus was in Glastonbury to visit the Tor and the Abbey ruins, just like many tourists still do. When they had seen all the town had to offer, Jesus was given the map and tasked with directing the boat back home. Jesus, though, was intrigued to see how close they were to Clevedon. He was a keen open water swimmer and had grown up swimming in the waters of the Sea of Galilee. He was aware of Clevedon's reputation as a centre of open water swimming and was keen to visit the lake. He had heard the stories of how the town's folk had bravely fought off the Welsh invaders centuries previously and was keen to visit the spot where it had all happened.

Joseph of Arimathea had no interest in swimming and was not keen to extend the trip. He refused Jesus's request to travel to Clevedon and the boat set sail for the Middle East. However, that night in a dream, the Angel Gabriel visited Joseph. Joseph was told, in no uncertain terms, that Jesus was the Son of God and he would do whatever Jesus requested. If he refused to do so then he would burn in hell for eternity. Joseph awoke from his sleep immediately and demanded that the boat turn around and head for Clevedon.

The boat arrived at Clevedon Pill the next evening. It was already getting dark and they received a warm welcome from locals who were delighted to have the Son of God visit their small fishing village. The party were invited to spend the night in the fort on Wain's Hill and there was much merriment. Jesus asked the locals about the lake but they were sad to report that it had fallen into a state of disrepair due to lack of government funding. There had been a huge storm a few years previously and the sea wall had collapsed. As a result, the lake was gone and there was nothing left for Jesus to see. The locals said that all was not lost. They were still able to swim in the sea at high tide and they were planning a sea swim the next morning at 8am. Jesus was invited to join them.

Jesus awoke early the next morning with a sore head. The walk across a windswept Poet's Walk did him the world of good. It wasn't long before he arrived at the site of what had once been the finest tidal pool in England. Jesus was sad to see what had happened to the lake and he was desperate to help the local folk who had been so welcoming towards him and Joseph. He told the locals to shut their eyes in prayer. When Jesus had finished leading them in prayer, he asked them to open their eyes. When they did, they could not believe what they saw. Not only was the lake fully restored, but Jesus was walking across the surface of the water. At first, they thought he must have been on top of the pontoon but they soon realised that the pontoon hadn't been built yet. In any case, there wasn't an overtopping tide so the pontoon would not have been hiding under the surface of the water, even if it had existed.

It is believed that these were the first miracles performed by Jesus. He is thought to have spent about two weeks in Clevedon, fishing and swimming in the lake, before he returned to Judea to fully begin his work as the Messiah. He founded a small chapel on the site of what is now St Andrew's church. It is believed that it was built as a fishing chapel and is thought to be the site of the oldest Christian church in Western Europe. However, this record has never been verified and the Guinness Book of Records refuses to recognise Clevedon's claim.

Joseph of Arimathea returned to the South West after Jesus's crucifixion and resurrection. He brought the Holy Grail with him and, according to folklore, it was buried in Glastonbury. However, a number of scholars now believe that it was buried in Clevedon, probably on the top of Wain's Hill. Nobody knows the exact location and we will probably never find out for certain. Wain's Hill is a protected historic monument. Any digging on the site, without permission, would be illegal.

Jesus never returned to Clevedon in the flesh, but he is in every one of us and he is as present in Clevedon now as he was on that visit about two thousand years ago.

ALFRED THE GREAT AND THE VIKINGS

Alfred the Great is recognised as one of the greatest and bravest of all the English kings. He visited Clevedon on two occasions. His first visit saw him leave in disgrace, but his second saw him leave the town a hero.

Alfred was a keen open water swimmer. On most mornings, he could be found taking a dip in the River Itchen in his hometown of Winchester. As king, he was required to travel throughout his kingdom. On his journeys, he always tried to visit local swimming spots.

He had important business in Clevedon in 872AD, not long after he had ascended to the throne. He ensured that he had enough spare time to visit the marine lake for a dip and the local swimmers were very honoured to have him join them. As he was new to the throne, Alfred was eager to get the locals on side. He knew that open water swimmers love nothing more than a slice or two of cake after their swims, so he decided to bake some cakes to take along. He spent the previous evening lovingly preparing them, but disaster struck when he fell asleep and the cakes burnt. He managed to rescue them before they were completely destroyed but they didn't look or smell good.

The next morning, Alfred made his way to a local shop, hoping to buy a packet of Malted Milk biscuits. Sadly, for Alfred, they had sold out. In desperation, Alfred packed the burnt cakes into his swim bag and headed for the lake. After a lovely swim, Alfred passed the cakes around. The local swimmers were insulted. He was told, in no uncertain terms, that he was no longer welcome at the lake and was asked to leave Clevedon immediately. The people of Clevedon no longer had any respect for Alfred, He was no king of theirs.

Alfred had the chance to restore his good name in Clevedon five years later.

The Vikings had been doing their best to seize control of Wessex, but Alfred's forces kept the Nordic invaders at bay. In 877AD, the Vikings decided that their best chance was to invade Wessex by sea. They already had bases in South West Wales and they sailed their longboats up the Bristol Channel, with Clevedon their target. They planned to arrive under the cover of darkness and catch the Clevedon folk unaware. Unbeknown to the Vikings, Alfred had spies in their camp and he knew of their plans.

The Vikings arrived in Clevedon on a late October evening, sailing silently into the shore. They planned to invade just before dawn the next morning. Alfred, though, had other plans. He had an entire army waiting for them on the Salthouse fields with hundreds of soldiers lined up behind the upper sea wall with bows and arrows at the ready.

As dawn approached, the Vikings left the relative safety of their longboats to be met by a wall of arrows. Knowing they had no chance of fighting this, the survivors fled back to their boats and tried to sail away. The Vikings were no fans of cold-water swimming and they did not know about the lake. Inadvertently, they had sailed over the sea wall on an overtopping tide. The tide had since gone out and they were now trapped. To make matters worse, Alfred had pulled the plug out and the water levels in the lake were now falling. After a couple of hours, there was no water left and the boats were stuck in the infamous Clevedon mud.

The few surviving Vikings were surrounded. They had no chance. Arrows of fire were aimed towards the boats which soon went up in flames. As the Vikings fled from the burning boats, they were met by more arrows. By mid-morning, every one of the Vikings lay dead. The Wessex army did not have a single casualty.

In a matter of hours, Alfred had gone from the town's most hated figure to a hero. The town folk were very grateful for his efforts in saving them from rape and pillage and he was invited to join them for a swim in the, now, replenished lake. Alfred was told he was welcome back for a swim anytime he wanted, on the condition that he never bought a cake with him.

Sadly, he never had the opportunity to visit Clevedon again but he is remembered fondly in the town to this very day.

WALTON-SUPER-MARE

We have all heard of Weston-Super-Mare, but most Clevedon locals will scratch their heads if you ask them where Walton-Super-Mare is. This is despite the fact that the historic village which is mentioned in the Domesday Book, is within the modern-day boundaries of Clevedon. It has a fascinating history going back well over a thousand years.

You have probably passed the lovely Church of St Mary's in Walton on the way to do a Ladye Bay swim. How many of us, though, have given this place more than a second glance? The Church. as we know it today, is a Gothic revival structure built in Victorian times, but it was actually built into the ruins of a much older building which dated back to the 13th century. Known as the Church of St Paul, the building was at the centre of the village of Walton-Super-Mare. The settlement pre-dates the church. A well in the grounds of the churchyard actually dates back to Anglo-Saxon times. It has recently been uncovered and is well worth a visit for those interested in local history.

The village was mysteriously abandoned in the early 17th century The church slowly fell into a state of disrepair and it lay in ruins before the previously mentioned restoration in the 19th century.

Whilst the reasons for the village's abandonment are not documented, archaeological discoveries in Victorian times give us clues. When the beach at Ladye Bay was allocated as a bathing spot for women, it was necessary to build a set of steps down to the beach. The beach had previously only been accessible by boat and it was assumed that had always been the case. However, during the works, traces of a previous set of steps were discovered. It was clear that these steps had been through much extensive restoration over the years, but, remarkably, parts of the steps were able to be dated back to the 9th century AD.

Historians believe that the settlement of Walton-Super-Mare was built where it was because of the excellent location for wild swimming. The sheltered bay provided a safe spot for a dip, especially as lifeboats had not yet been invented. Villagers probably made the short walk down from the top of the hill to have a swim at high tide when sea conditions were suitable. No evidence exists to suggest they would have swum down to what is now the pier beach. Betty and Mildred are still believed to be the first people to have attempted that swim.

It is believed that the steps collapsed in the 17th century (probably due to a mighty storm) at about the same time that the village was abandoned. The steps were probably too expensive to repair. With no other easily accessible wild swimming facilities nearby, it is thought that the villagers probably relocated to Clevedon which was more swimmer friendly. The marine lake (which, like Walton-Super-Mare is mentioned in the Domesday Book) was accessible at all times (apart from during drainages to clear out mud in the spring and autumn). Clevedon expanded in the 19th century to include the site of the old church which was restored to serve a new local population.

In 1965, an archaeological dig was held close to the churchyard on what was believed to be the site of the old village. Many fascinating artefacts were discovered including numerous items of swimming gear. Swimming costumes and goggles were discovered aplenty but, perhaps most incredibly, a number of snorkels (some over a thousand years old) were found. Snorkels are never used at Clevedon these days due to the murky nature of the water.

Some scientists believe that the discovery of the snorkels suggests the water was much clearer one thousand years ago. There are ongoing studies at Bristol University researching this.

Very few traces of Walton-St -Mary remain today. It is worth reflecting on this wonderful history on your next visit to Ladye Bay though. It is remarkable to think that when you swim here, that you are doing exactly what people were doing here, more than a thousand years ago.

GERTRUDE'S CHILDHOOD

"I was born in the town of Clevedon on the 25th of September 1912. My mother, Hetty and father, Stanley, were not wealthy but my eleven siblings and I never wanted for anything. We all made the most of the outdoor lives we were able to lead, due to being brought up in a seaside town. I was the third youngest so I always had older siblings around to keep an eye on me and to smack me one if I dared to misbehave.

Swimming was always a major part of my childhood. We would swim regularly in the marine lake and it was almost unheard of for a day to go by without a Higginbottom entering the water. My older siblings had taught me to swim from a very young age and I took to it like a duck to water. I don't remember it myself, but I am told that I did my first swim to the pontoon a day before my second birthday. Unfortunately, I was too tired to swim back, but I was able to hitch a lift on a paddle board. By my fourth birthday, I was swimming circuits of the lake. It is no surprise that I went on to make such a name for myself as a swimmer.

I have no real memories of the Great War. I had only recently turned six when it ended and the war had more or less passed Clevedon by. Of course, we had no TV then to keep up with what was going on, although I do have vague memories of my father tuning into the radio for updates. My father never went to fight in Europe. He was well into his forties when the war began. He spent most of the next few years stationed on the top of Wain's Hill, with a pair of binoculars on the lookout for German warships. The Germans were known to have their eyes on the marine lake. The worry was that they might invade at night and, when swimmers turned up for their early morning dips, they would find German towels filling the side of the lake denying the local swimmers access to the water. My father had always said that dryrobes were a load of nonsense and, religiously, refused to wear one. However, he was more than happy to wear my mother's robe, on those long, cold, wet nights on the top of Wain's Hill.

One of my most vivid early memories came on my 7th birthday. To my great surprise, and pleasure, I received a dryrobe and a tow float. I have no idea how my parents could afford such expensive gifts. I do, however, remember my father telling me I had an extraordinary talent for open water swimming and that I now had the necessary tools to make an impression. If there had been no World War then it's highly unlikely that my father would have been persuaded to buy me a dryrobe. Without the dryrobe, I would have not have been as successful as I was. The Great War was not all bad.

I wrote this poem on my 7th birthday. Not bad for my age, I feel.

Birthday Gifts

When I opened my presents
On my birthday today
I could not believe what
I'd been given, no way
No toys for this youngster
Nor a book to be read
Nor some shoes for my feet
Nor some sweets to be fed
For instead I was gifted
And I don't wish to gloat
An amazing new dryrobe
And an orange tow float.

Almost all of the next couple of years were spent either at school or at the lake. I was not allowed to swim in the winter months. My father would not let me wear a wetsuit as he said they were for wimps. He said that no son or daughter of his would ever be seen in one. At the time, I was very annoyed with what I saw as being a silly rule. Now, though, I am grateful for what he did for me. To this day, I have never worn a wetsuit and I refuse to even talk to someone if I see them wearing one.

Nevertheless, I spent many hours watching those brave women (always women) swimming in the lake every winter. Wild swimming was massive in the 1920s and 30s although it would go out of fashion afterwards. My parents said I was too young and did not have the required body fat to swim in the winter months, although I was a regular swimmer at Strode Leisure Centre. I used to love the brightly coloured swimming costumes worn by the women at the lake which contrasted with their black dryrobes (you could only get them in black in those days). I longed for the warmth of spring and the chance to get back in the water.

My swimming kept on improving until, one very special day in May 1922, my father spoke some words to me which I will never forget.

"Gertrude, my dear. I am taking you on your very first sea swim".

THE INVENTION OF THE YO-YO

Gertrude tells the fascinating story of how the yo-yo was invented in Clevedon.

I have vivid memories from my childhood of a close friend of my father, a Mr. Arthur Bartholomew. Mr. Bartholomew (as he was known to me and my friends), was a keen swimmer in the marine lake back in the 1920s. He was a retired chap with a rather splendid moustache and he spent much of his time designing some truly wonderful children's toys. My friends and I spent many happy days trying out his latest inventions but, sadly, his toys never sold beyond the local shops in Clevedon town centre and on Hill Road. That said, he did get a couple of his toys put on sale in the middle aisle of the LIDL store down by the Curzon cinema.

Mr. Bartholomew (as he was known to me and my friends), had spent many happy hours observing the huge tides of the Severn Estuary and the Bristol Channel. He had an idea to develop a toy which would bounce up and down and mimic the Clevedon tides. We spent many happy hours playing on Marshalls Field trying out the various prototypes of this new toy. Some of us mastered it in no time at all, but others (myself included) could never get the hang of it. There was no doubt that this new toy was going to make Mr. Bartholomew (as he was known to me and my friends) incredibly rich.

We all struggled to come up with a name for the new toy, but my friend, Muriel, came up with the name which we all know to this day. Given the many hours we had spent on Marshalls Field playing with this new toy, she thought up the name, Yeo-Yeo, in recognition of the two River Yeos which form the boundary to the north and south of the field.

Sadly Mr. Bartholomew (as he was known to me and my friends) died suddenly the day after Muriel came up with the name and he was unable to enjoy the success of his new invention. As his design had not been patented, his family did not enjoy the riches which the Yeo-Yeo should have brought them as toy companies from far and wide ripped off the design.

Nowadays, every child has a yo-yo (the name was changed as the manufacturers thought it sounded cooler and would appeal more to the kids), but how many of them are aware of the fascinating story behind their invention and of the tidal range which gave Mr. Bartholomew (as he was known to me and my friends) the idea to come up with this ever-popular toy?

I wrote this poem about my failed attempts to master the yo-yo.

Yo-yo

> Like the channel where we dip
> The yo-yo has us in her grip
> Up and down the yo-yo goes
> She starts high then falls to our toes
> And just like that, she bounces back
> But sadly, I don't have the knack
> My yo-yo skills aren't very good
> I really, really wish I could
> Make her return up high again
> But. sadly, all my tries in vain.

GERTRUDE'S FIRST SEA SWIM

My first sea swim was certainly an eye opener.

Until now, I had only swum in the lake. Ninety percent of the swimmers at the lake were middle-aged women in dryrobes, but my first trip to the beach was a very different experience. There was not a dryrobe in sight and the people were nowhere near as friendly. My father explained why.

"These people have been swimming in the sea for years, long before it became trendy. They detest this new trend and hate having to share the water with this new wave of 'wild swimmers', a phrase they detest. They have no time for newcomers, Gertie. Don't worry though. In about ten years they will probably learn to accept you and they may even let you join their club and use their cave".

There were three 'caves' at the beach. The enormous one at the end, down by Pissy Corner, was used by the Sailing Club for boat storage. Then there was a tiny one, at the other end, which was used by myself and my father that day. It was only a few feet deep and was open to the elements if we got a westerly wind. The cave in the middle was much roomier and was used by members of the swimming club. You did not dare to even walk past their cave unless you were a member.

My father had been a member of their club but was expelled one day when he turned up wearing a dryrobe. He had become rather attached to wearing one after his war time experiences and decided to wear it to the beach one day, when it was raining. He was kicked out of the club immediately, with no right to appeal. None of them ever spoke a word to him again.

I was very jealous of their changing space. I hoped one day I would be able to join them as it looked much roomier and warmer than our cave. Thankfully, my father had chosen a warm and sunny day for my first sea swim, but there would be countless occasions in the future when it would be wet and windy. My father announced that it was time to get into the water and we would swim out to the first pier leg.

I found the entry across the pebbles to be a little painful. Thankfully, it was a spring tide, so we didn't have to walk far. My father pointed out the slipway which, he said, we could use to enter the water on neap tides. I dived straight into the water, unable to contain my excitement. Immediately, I knew that this was a completely different experience to swimming in the lake.

We had a fairly uneventful swim to the first pier leg and back, probably exactly what my father had planned for my first sea swim. As we arrived at the pier, I looked up to Ladye Bay and thought of Betty and Mildred and their epic swim. From that point on, I was determined that I would one day complete the Ladye Bay swim. We noticed the friars getting out at the Monk's Steps after serving their morning penance. I had heard the story of their daily swims many times, but I had never truly believed it until I saw it with my own eyes.

My father said we must return to the beach. The tide had now turned and we risked being swept down to the lake if we waited much longer. I would have liked to have swum out to the second or third leg, but he insisted that I would have to wait for another day. Part of me was disappointed, but I was only nine years old. I knew there would be many more opportunities. Indeed, that stretch of sea would go on to dominate my life. I was hooked.

BETTY AND MILDRED

Many regular Clevedon swimmers have completed the famous Ladye Bay to pier swim. What a lot of people don't know is that the Ladye Bay swim has a fascinating history going back to Victorian times.

Clevedon began to gain popularity as a coastal resort with the opening of the Clevedon branch line in 1847. Thousands would visit Clevedon to take in the sights and sounds which included the now famous pier which was built in the 1860s. Sea bathing became popular during this time and many swam off the main beach by the pier. Sadly, women were excluded from participating as it was considered highly inappropriate for women and men to swim together at this time.

In 1873, the decision was taken to open a new beach at North Clevedon Bay. The beach was considered ideal for women only bathing, due to its secluded and sheltered location. The beach was renamed Ladies Bay and, soon, women were able to enjoy the health benefits of open water swimming. In order to protect the safety of the women, a viewing platform was built to the south of the beach so that responsible males could keep an eye on the swimmers. However, it was not long before this became a popular venue for moustached Victorian men with binoculars to take the opportunity to perv on the women in the hope of catching the occasional glimpse of an ankle. This viewing platform is still there today and is well worth a visit for those interested in local history.

The new beach was not popular with all. Mr. William Samuels wrote to the Charlcombe Chime to express his disapproval.

"A beach for women at North Clevedon Bay (I refuse to use the new name)? Women do not have time for this tomfoolery. They should be at home looking after their families, not engaging in these activities. My wife and daughters have been told, in no uncertain terms, that they will not be visiting this beach. They know they have no alternative but to obey me".

There were further complaints in the Portbury Portal. Mr. Alan Pervington was unhappy with the new arrangement.

"I went down to the new viewing point at North Clevedon Bay to see what exactly was going on. The place was full of men watching the semi-naked women through their binoculars. Luckily, I had packed my binoculars as well and I was able to have a good, long look at what was taking place. I have never seen so much female flesh on display. After a couple of hours, I had seen enough and went home in disgust".

In the late 19th century, the suffragist movement was becoming increasingly popular and many women were feeling unhappy that they were excluded from swimming by the pier. A plan was hatched by two brave women, Mildred Summerhayes and Betty Wright. They would swim down from Ladye Bay, naked as the day they were born, and exit the water on their arrival at the pier beach. The nakedness was a protest at the fact that women were expected to swim in uncomfortable bathing suits which covered their whole bodies. Sadly, Betty drowned somewhere by the hotel but Mildred made it all the way to the beach. Her arrival caused a right commotion, as you can probably imagine. Mildred, though, was unperturbed and calmly exited the water before embarking on the walk back to Ladies Bay to collect her stuff. Sadly, she did not have room for her dryrobe and flask in her tow float and she was forced to make the walk back in her birthday suit. She passed away on the way back to Ladies Bay due to hypothermia.

The responses to the swim varied immensely. Many were delighted that they had died in their attempt and hoped it would put others off. Some men, however, were more supportive of their efforts. A Mr. Horace Major wrote to the Tickenham Star to show his support.

"I enjoyed the sight of the naked woman walking up the pier beach after her swim down from Ladies Bay. I fully support their movement and hope that many more women will do the same. I will happily welcome them at the beach and keep a close eye on them afterwards to make sure they do not succumb to hypothermia".

Betty and Mildred were not forgotten and many women were inspired to follow their example. There are over one hundred recorded examples of women completing this swim over the next ten years and, no doubt, countless others that we don't know about. Clevedon Town Council were eventually forced to bow to pressure and both beaches were opened up to one and all (apart from dogs on the pier beach which are still banned to this day).

Over the following decades, the Ladye Bay (it is not known exactly when or why the name was changed) swim became increasingly popular, almost exclusively with women. Sadly, the intervention of war in 1939 meant women had more important things to be getting on with and open water swimming ceased to be a major leisure activity until Wim Hof reintroduced it during the COVID lockdown in 2020.

Nowadays, the Ladye Bay swim is especially popular in the summer months. You will often see the sight of tow floats bobbing up and down in the sea close to high tide. It is a rewarding swim for those with the necessary swimming capabilities and stamina but is not one to be undertaken lightly.

THE MONKS' STEPS

The Monks' Steps are one of Clevedon's hidden secrets. Very little is known about their history, but it is believed their existence is linked to the friary of the Church of the Immaculate Conception, not far from the top of the steps. Many Ladye Bay swimmers will be familiar with this church, as it is a major landmark on the popular Ladye Bay swim.

When a group of French Franciscan friars came to Somerset in 1880, the Bishop of Clifton suggested they should locate in Clevedon. A mission was started in 1882 and the friary, as we know it today, was begun in 1886. The first foundation stone was laid on 16/2/1886 and the Church was opened and consecrated on 14/7/1887.

Of course, this was the time when the Ladye Bay swim was gaining in popularity following the exploits of Betty and Mildred. Like all monks and friars, they would spend their days praying, eating porridge and feeling miserable, but the friars in Clevedon are also known to have developed a love of open water swimming.

Every day, at high tide, the friars would march to Ladye Bay, get in the water and swim naked to the pier. They would do this regardless of conditions or the time of year. This would lead to much suffering on their part. It was seen as a way of making a sacrifice to atone for their sins.

The friars were not permitted to use tow floats or to wear dryrobes on their exit from the water. These were seen as a way of alleviating suffering and would make the swim much less of a sacrifice. They were, therefore, forced to make the walk back to the friary completely naked.

The pier beach was very popular with swimmers at this time. It was considered somewhat unkempt for the friars to be seen exiting the water in this undignified manner, in front of hordes of holidaymakers and day trippers. However, to stop this daily swim would be seen as disappointing God so an alternative plan was developed.

It was decided that a set of steps would be built into the cliff below the friary. This shortened the swim by about a quarter of a mile. This was not considered to be a bad thing as a number of friars had perished due to the length of the swim in the winter months. The steps provided a suitable and private exit point for the brave friars, away from the prying eyes of the public.

If you have ever visited the Monks' Steps, you will know how dangerous the descent looks from the top. The steps, however, were only designed to be climbed from the bottom. To go down the steps was said to be' a fast route to Heaven'. Thankfully, there are no known instances of anybody falling to their death on the steps.

The tradition of the friar's daily swim declined over time. It became a weekly event over the summer months, during the 1930s, but it stopped altogether during the war and never resumed. The steps, however, remain as a memorial to the brave monks and friars who swam and, sometimes, perished in the treacherous cold waters of Clevedon on the Ladye Bay swim.

GERTRUDE AND THE STEPS

Gertrude Higginbottom was known for her sense of adventure but even she was not a fan of the Monks' Steps. The steps, nowadays, are overgrown and almost impossible to find. Even in Gertrude's day, they were incredibly treacherous. She only stood at the top of the steps once and was not inclined to attempt the descent. She wrote this poem about her experience.

The Monks' Steps

I've passed them many times below
To swim past fast, the way to go
No need to leave the sea quite yet
The swim beyond is not a threat
Head for the beach and exit there
Out of the sea without a care
But holy men had no such choice
To them the swim was to rejoice
Then, up to pray in church above
Their sacrifice to show God's love.
Atop Monks' Steps I one time stood
I knew then that I never would
Descend those steps down to the shore
The fear of falling chilled my core
The monks, they climbed, again, again
In awe of God, those holy men.

GERTRUDE'S FIRST LADYE BAY SWIM

Gertrude remembers her first Ladye Bay swim.

When I went downstairs for my breakfast, on my twelfth birthday, my father was waiting for me in the kitchen.

"Happy Birthday, Gertrude dear. We shall eat our breakfast and then you shall go upstairs and pack your swimming gear. We are going to Ladye bay".

"You mean", I stuttered. I could not get the words out of my mouth.

"Yes dear. We shall be swimming from Ladye Bay to the pier. We shall be following all those who have done it before, including Betty and Mildred and the friars of the Church of the Immaculate Conception."

Betty and Mildred were my all-time heroes. I could not believe that I would be doing the very swim which they had invented a few decades previously. I don't remember what I had for breakfast that day but I remember everything about the swim.

We walked to the pier. I had packed my dryrobe, my tow float and my swim shoes. My father did not have any of those things. He was old school and he was also a deeply religious man. He wanted to follow the example of the friars, who swam without any of those luxuries. I don't know how he managed to walk across the pebbles in bare feet. Even with my swim shoes on my feet suffered.

We put our stuff in the cave and set off on the walk to Ladye Bay. My father had never swum one-way before, but he knew I wasn't ready to swim two-ways and he wanted to accompany me on the walk up. I enjoyed the walk although, I have to admit, I was a tad nervous. I was fully aware that Betty and Mildred did not survive the swim and I was worried in case I followed in their footsteps. My father was a good judge, though, and would not have taken me if he had any doubts.

This was the first time I had done this walk. My father pointed out some landmarks on the way up. He showed me the path down to Monks' Steps (which looked incredibly dangerous) and the viewing platform which looks down onto Ladye Bay. This was where men had stood, looking through binoculars to see the women in their bathing costumes, when it was a female only beach.

After walking for about twenty minutes, we arrived at Ladye Bay. We got ready for the swim. I packed and blew up my tow float. My father left his stuff on the beach and said he would run back up afterwards to collect his belongings. He then said a prayer, thanking Betty and Mildred for creating this swim, praying for their souls and, finally, praying that we would complete the swim safely.

Then it was time. We got into the water. It was late September and the sea was still warm. I only wore my costume, goggles, swim hat and swim shoes. Sadly, earplugs were yet to be invented. This was going to cause me problems in later life, but the young, adventurous Gertrude didn't worry about things like that. I thought I would be young forever. I had my tow float with my clothes in and my towel and dryrobe would be waiting for me at the other end in the cave.

We started slowly. My father wanted me to take in the view down to the pier, which I duly did. It looked a long way away. After a bit of heads-up breaststroke, we put our heads down in the water and started to swim front crawl. About ten minutes later we reached the Walton Bay Hotel. My father knew I would want to stop here. I paused to remember Betty who had drowned here all those years previously. It had been a very stormy day when she lost her life but, today, the water was completely calm. After a couple of minutes of quiet contemplation, we set off again with the pier now firmly in our sights.

Sadly, Betty and Mildred were not the last to lose their lives on this swim. Indeed, it is thought that the number of fatalities on this stretch of water over the years was well in excess of one hundred. Many were keen to complete this historic swim but were not strong enough swimmers to do so. Many set off when the sea was too rough, whilst others misjudged the tide times and were swept past the pier, never to be seen again.

Thankfully, there were no such dangers for us. My father had purchased the Clevedon Herald that morning to check the tide times and the weather forecast. Conditions were perfect and the swim passed without incident. I actually found it to be incredibly easy.

The current really picked up once we had passed the hotel. We were going so fast that I missed the Monks' Steps (I had been very keen to see them). Before we knew it, we were being swept under the pier. Here, the current was at its strongest. It would have been impossible to swim against it, even for a moment. I thought, for a brief time, that we were going to be swept past the slipway, but the current eased considerably and we made it to our planned exit point without incident.

We had done it! We got out onto the slipway and returned to the cave. I quickly dried myself off and put on my dryrobe. I felt so proud. I was now a fully qualified Clevedon swimmer.

A MERE WOMAN

Gertrude Higginbottom remembers the first ever successful Bristol Channel crossing by a swimmer.

On the 5th of September, 1927, three weeks before my 15th birthday, something happened which would change my life.

I often looked out across the Bristol Channel when I swam at Clevedon marine lake. Wales didn't look that far away. I dreamt of being the first person to swim across the channel. I was young and naive and I believed the swim looked fairly straightforward.

Of course, it was nowhere near as easy as it looked. The estuary has the second highest tidal range in the world and the currents made it extremely dangerous to swim across and, potentially, deadly. Many men had attempted the swim and all had failed miserably. Many experts believed that the swim was impossible and that it would never be completed.

When it was announced that Kathleen Thomas was going to attempt the swim, I was extremely excited. Most of my friends had posters of the latest pop stars up on their bedroom walls, but I had posters of Kathleen. The idea that she might become the first person to swim across the Bristol Channel, beating all the men to the prize, was one which inspired me greatly. My father, though, found the idea hilarious. "No woman could ever manage that swim. I will be amazed if she even gets to halfway", he said to me. I had many arguments with him about this. I was convinced she would succeed. He told me that I was young and naive and that I would soon grow out of it.

On the 5th of September, the 21-year-old Kathleen Thomas set off from Penarth. I remember watching her launch herself into the muddy depths of the Bristol Channel that morning on BBC Breakfast. There were thousands lining the Penarth sea-front to wave her off. Sadly, for me, she was swimming to Weston-Super-Mare, rather than Clevedon. I asked my father to take me to Weston, so that we could watch her arrive, but he refused. He said there was no possibility of her making a successful crossing and he wasn't going to waste his time, or mine, travelling to Weston for no reason.

I was furious. This was my chance to witness history being made and he wanted to deny me that opportunity. Luckily, my friend Johnny was travelling down with his parents and I was offered a lift. Johnny was almost as excited as I was. Unfortunately, his flatulence was especially bad that day and the journey to Weston was not a pleasant one.

It wasn't long after we arrived at Weston that we spotted the support boat, about a mile off shore. We couldn't see Kathleen (the use of tow floats was not permitted so she wasn't visible from such a distance), but we knew she must be swimming alongside the boat. Everyone was very excited; she was within touching distance of making history. The crowd was enormous. Many of the older male spectators were scoffing at her attempt, suggesting that she had probably had a ride on the boat for most of the journey. Others were still saying she wouldn't make it. The misogyny was horrendous.

That final mile seemed to last forever. Through my binoculars, I could see her stroke was shortening. She looked exhausted. Thankfully, she was getting closer and closer and the sight of land surely gave her a lot of encouragement. As she got closer still, she would have heard the roars of support from the crowd, They were absolutely deafening. Eventually, she made it! As I watched her walk out of the water, I sent my father a text to gloat. "Father, just to let you know, a woman has become the first person to swim across the Bristol Channel". He replied and admitted he had been wrong. He had watched the swim on live TV and had been cheering her on. Much later, my mother told me he had got more and more excited the closer she got to the finish, and that he had a tear in his eye as she got out of the water. I had never seen my father cry and I never would, but my mother swore that it happened.

'A mere woman' had conquered the Bristol Channel", as a newspaper headline announced the next morning. The world was watching on in amazement.

Two years later, Edith Parnell, who was a fierce rival of mine in club events, became the second person to successfully cross the channel. She was only 16 years old and remains the youngest person to make this crossing, Edith took three hours longer than Kathleen Thomas, but it was still an incredible achievement. This time, my father took me to Weston to see her complete the swim. She looked very cold as she exited the water, I was very honoured to hand over her dryrobe as she walked up the beach. We had been rivals in the pool but we became great friends, often completing long swims together in the channel. I was delighted when she told me she was pregnant. When she died in childbirth in 1935, I was absolutely devastated and I have missed her every day since.

Kathleen and Edith inspired me to become the swimmer I became. To see women being the pioneers in my sport meant so much to me. I have no idea who the first man to swim the channel was. The fact is that, by then, nobody really cared. The women had shown the men who ruled the water. I would go on to complete the channel swim myself, this time landing in Clevedon. I got a great welcome as I walked up the slipway, but my swim was a mere footnote to the women who had led the way, several years before.

Kathleen

A mere woman they said you were
But still, you showed the men who's boss
I always had belief in you
Not all believed, but that's their loss
Go on brave Kathleen, swim from Wales
Prove to the men that women rule
The first to beat those deadly tides
They called you a deluded fool
Now look who has egg on their face
Those jealous men did not believe
So happy that you proved them wrong
'A mere woman'- well, how naive!

PERVERTS' PERCH

Gertrude tells us about the building of Perverts' Perch.

The lake was extensively restored in 1928. It was closed for most of the year whilst restoration took place. At the time, Poets' Walk was becoming very popular with walkers. Part of the restoration scheme involved building a viewing platform above the deep end where walkers could take in views of the pier.

This was not the first time such a structure had been built in Clevedon. The viewing platform to the south of Ladye Bay was built so that men could keep an eye on the women bathing at the beach to ensure they remained safe. However, it was not long before the platform started to attract men with binoculars hoping to view the women in their bathing costumes. In prudish Victorian times, the sight of a woman in a bathing costume was a rare treat for sex starved men and it is no surprise that this spot became so popular.

The new viewing platform at the lake provided wonderful views, but not, as had been intended, of the pier. As it directly overlooks the spot where most bathers get dressed, it was no surprise that it soon gained the nickname, 'Perverts' Perch'.

Myself and my female friends felt uncomfortable with this new arrangement. The men above would pretend they were looking across to the pier, but we all knew what they were really up to. Thank goodness we had our dryrobes to change under! On warmer days, though, our dryrobes were left at home and we had to fidget about under our towels, knowing that the slightest mistake would give our audience a surprise treat.

However, as time went on, we became less and less conscious of the men watching from above. We were happy to give them the occasional flash of a bit of corset. Of course, what was considered a flash back then would be considered to be no such thing nowadays. That said, a flash of our admittedly modest underwear would send men into a state of ecstasy. It was not uncommon for men to become over-excited and become unwell. One man got so excited that he suffered a heart attack and fell from the wall. He missed landing on a friend of mine by mere inches. He broke his neck on impact and was killed instantly. We didn't tell his wife what he was up to as a mark of respect.

I have happy memories of my younger days changing here. Nowadays, as an elderly-women, nobody gives me a second glance.

I was overjoyed to find this lovely poem I wrote back in my youth recalling my experiences at the lake.

Perverts' Perch

The perverts are a-perving
On the ladies getting dressed
But for us it doesn't matter
And, indeed, we feel we're blessed
As we really like to flaunt it
And of this we feel so sure
When bikinis are invented
We shall flaunt it even more.

JOHNN̲Y

Gertrude Higginbottom remembers a very dear friend of hers.

I have known some remarkable swimmers in my time, but none more so than the incredible Johnny Guffington. I went to school with Johnny. He was in the year above me but, as we swam together in the school swimming team, we got to know each other very well. Johnny was a very talented swimmer and won numerous regional championships, but he could never make the step up to national level.

Johnny was a lovely guy but, it has to be said, he did have a problem with flatulence. You didn't want to be anywhere near him on one of his bad days. I remember that one day he did the loudest bottom burp you have ever heard in the school swimming pool. The whole building had to be evacuated.

Johnny's ascent into swimming stardom began one day at the annual school talent contest. At the time, none of us realised how this would help his swimming. I remember he performed a lovely rendition of farts to the tune of the Dryrobe Song. All of the children went wild with appreciation, but some of the more conservative teachers were not so impressed. To the disappointment of all the children, he was disqualified. There would have been a riot but, again, the building had to be evacuated due to the smell. It was so bad that we all forgot about the injustice.

However, his ability to time his farts so well was to make him famous. In 1927 he had won the regional championships as usual and progressed to the national championships in London. I was in attendance myself, having qualified in a couple of events. The final of the 100 metres freestyle went, for the most part, as planned. Johnny, once again, could not cope with the step up in grade and he was trailing in 6th place as they entered the final 20 metres.

Then the unexpected happened. Out of nowhere, a deafening sound erupted out of Johnny's bottom. The strength of the fart propelled him forward so much that it moved him from 6th to 1st place in no time at all. He won the race and a new star was born. Sadly, for me, I never got to race in those championships. Johnny had followed through and the pool had to be closed for 24 hours to be cleaned. The remainder of the championships were abandoned.

Thankfully, Johnny was able to perfect his technique to ensure that he didn't follow through again. This also made his farts more efficient and more powerful. Over the next few months, Johnny got faster and faster and he progressed beyond his own age group to win the all-aged national championships and qualify to represent Great Britain in the 1928 Olympics, which were to be held in Amsterdam.

Johnny was a massive favourite for the Olympic title and he was the talk of the swimming world. Unfortunately, he never got to compete for the gold medal. The IOC had been following his exploits closely and declared that bottom burps in the pool were now against the rules. All of Johnny's times were removed from the record books. He was not banned from competing, but, unable to fart in the water, he returned to racing at mainly regional level.

The story did not end there though. Johnny had gained quite a following and he did a number of exhibition events at the lake. Thousands would turn up to watch him fart his way along the sea wall. One day he farted so strongly that he created a tsunami effect in the water. A number of spectators ended up in the lake as a consequence. Thankfully, they were all strong swimmers and no harm was done.

Unfortunately, Johnny's story did not have a happy ending. One day, he was training in Clevedon, when an unsuspecting passer-by tossed a cigarette end into the lake. Tragically, Johnny passed wind at exactly the same time that the cigarette end hit the water. I heard the explosion from my home on the other side of town. Johnny and the smoker were both killed instantly and a number of other swimmers suffered life changing injuries.

Johnny was a dear friend of mine and I have missed him every day since. That said, I am certain he would have enjoyed going out in the way he did- farting in Clevedon marine lake, his favourite place.

I wrote this poem to wish Johnny all the best in Amsterdam, just before the IOC decided to ban him from competing.

Go Johnny

Johnny, fart your way to glory
Make sure you let your bottom fling
You on your way to win that gold
To show the world just who is king
Be the first Olympic champion
To use his backside to win the race
But please, don't follow through my friend
Make sure you win that gold with grace.

THE DRYROBE SONG

The Dryrobe Song is a late 19th century folk song, believed to originate from Clevedon. The composer is unknown. The song deals with a new growth in 'wild swimming', which was becoming very popular at the time, largely influenced by the exploits of Betty and Mildred. I wrote about this song in my previous book, 'Sunrise', and told the story of how my grandmother used to sing it to me as a child.

As swimming outdoors became more and more popular, many old timers, who had been swimming in the sea for years, became more and more annoyed and frustrated. A Mr. Harry Tiddington wrote to the Clevedon Herald expressing his disgust.

"These middle-aged women come down to the lake at the height of summer, dressed in their dryrobes with their flasks of hot tea. I never wear my dryrobe until November at the earliest. Just what is the world coming to?"

A letter from Mrs. Ivy Ridlington in the Portishead Observer expressed similar concerns.

"I went to swim at Sugar Loaf this morning. Not only was the beach full of women in their dryrobes but I witnessed at least three swimmers in wetsuits and others in neoprene boots and gloves. I'm sure when I looked at the calendar this morning that it was June. Just what is the world coming to?"

There were further complaints about those who swim to boost their mental health. One anonymous source on an internet forum wrote.

"What is going on with all this talk of mental health? My father worked a sixty-hour week in the coal mines and, not once, did I hear him moaning about feeling depressed. People these days are too soft. I have been swimming for years for exercise, my mental health has never once been a consideration. Just what is the world coming to?".

The term 'wild swimming' was one which had caused a lot of controversy. Ethel Redbottom wrote to the Gordano Times.

"I have been swimming in the sea for my entire life. Now these newbies have invaded the sea from their chlorinated, indoor pools and coined the phrase, 'wild swimming'. I have never heard such nonsense in my life. They sit on the beach sipping at glasses of warm mulled wine after their swims. I have never seen mulled wine drunk out of the festive season before. Just what is the world coming to?"

This disgust at the new trend of 'wild swimming' in the late 19th century is almost certainly what led to the composition of the Dryrobe Song. The song was released as a single and reached number twelve in the national charts, despite most of the sales coming from the Clevedon and North Somerset area. Radio hadn't been invented in the late 19th century so it was hard for the song to gather any momentum nationally.

The Clevedon Times reported the following in 1897.

"The HMV store in Clevedon has been unable to cope with demand. Records have been flying off the shelves. When I went in this morning, there was not a single 7 inch available. I managed to get hold of the 12 inch and I really enjoyed the extended version when I listened to it when I got home".

Despite its chart success, it is not known who composed the song or who performed on the recording. Credited to 'The Dryrobers', there is no record of who was involved in this group and they never made another record together.

The song remained popular well into the 1930s. However, its popularity faded thereafter and it was only in the last couple of years that the song was rediscovered when I found a dusty old cassette dated from the 1930s which had belonged to my grandmother.

The Dryrobe Song is now staging a bit of a revival and is sung occasionally by swimmers to help them warm up after a cold-water swim. The lyrics are as follows.

The Dryrobe Song

Never must a dryrobe wear
Till Halloween is in the air
And never wear thine neoprene
Until Advent is on the scene

Thine bikini shan't get wet
She hasn't been invented yet
And skinny dipping thou shan't do
Enlightened times are far from you

Never leave thine litter strewn
Or bad tidings will fall on you
But filthy water we don't care
We swim in sewage, we're not scared

Never stress 'bout feeling down
Stiff upper lip or thou willst drown

We only dip post cleaning spree
Then home to cook our husband's tea

All thine cake shalt be homemade
That processed crap is years away
And only sip thine warm mulled wine
When it is almost Christmas time

Our cold swims are so much fun
The water is for everyone
But wild swimming thou shall not say
We called it swimming in my day.

GERTRUDE'S FIRST LOVE

Gertrude tells the story of a brief dalliance with a Hollywood star.

I met Archie at the lake one day in 1928. He was from Bristol and I was immediately struck by how handsome he was. I don't remember how we got chatting, but I remember that we swam two lengths together and had a lovely discussion about the joys of open water swimming. He told me he had only recently discovered the lake but, now he had found it, he was visiting from Bristol a couple of times a week.

When we had completed our swim, Archie asked me if I fancied grabbing a coffee in the Salty. I could not decline such an offer and one coffee soon turned into a long lunch on Walrus Terrace. Sadly, Archie had to return to Bristol eventually. He told me he had to get to his acting class at the Bristol Old Vic. We had spent so much time talking about swimming that this was the first I had heard of his acting ambitions.

It wasn't long before we were courting. My family all loved Archie and kept asking me when he was going to propose. One day we swam at the lake and Archie suggested we get out on the pontoon so we could dive in. It soon became apparent that diving was the last thing on his mind. On top of the pontoon, Archie got down on one knee and asked me to marry him. Of course, I said yes.

With a date set for the wedding, it was decided that we would live in Clevedon. I needed to be close to water as I was approaching the peak of my swimming powers. Archie was taking acting jobs intermittently and was offered a position as a pot washer at Teatro to work around his acting roles. They were very flexible and we found a small two-bedroom terrace which we would move into after the wedding.

We were very much in love but, a few days before the wedding, everything changed. Completely out of the blue, Archie was offered a job as a Hollywood film star. Teatro could not match what he could earn in Hollywood and he had to accept the job. He asked me to go with him. I was torn. I loved Archie but I also loved Clevedon. Archie said he would be flying to Hollywood the day after the wedding. He hoped that I would be on the plane with him

It was the hardest decision of my life but, in the end, I opted to stay in Clevedon. I was still only 19 and the thought of moving to Hollywood and leaving Clevedon behind terrified me. I could not deny Archie his opportunity. He had always wanted to make a career as a world-famous film star.

We spent one last day together in Clevedon. We did the Ladye Bay swim together for the one and only time, had lunch in Scarlett's and then said our goodbyes. We would never meet again.

I saw Archie on the screen at the Curzon many times. I was delighted to see him doing so well, but never regretted my decision. Six months later, I met the man who would be my husband and I knew I had made the correct choice. I'm sure that Archie felt the same way.

CLEVEDON PIER

We all love Clevedon Pier. Sir John Betjeman described it as the most beautiful pier in England and it's easy to see why. He even wrote a poem about it.

Oh, Clevedon Pier

Oh, Clevedon Pier, you warm my heart
I can't describe my love for thee
Whene'er I need to find some peace
I'll tread your boards, head out to sea
Up high I watch the swimmers pass
Their bravery I can't explain
The finest pier in this whole land
Her beauty will not ever wane.

The idea for a pier at Clevedon was first floated in 1861. Tourists were already making their way into Clevedon on the new railway line and it was thought that a pier would make Clevedon even more attractive to day trippers. The main reason for her creation was to give the swimmers something to swim around. The Ladye Bay swim had not been invented at this point and swimming at the beach was becoming a bit boring. It was decided that building a pier for swimmers to swim around would provide an exciting challenge and swimmers would be rewarded with a diving platform at the end of the pier for those who got that far. The legendary architect, Hans Price was commissioned to design the pier. Hans, a keen swimmer himself (although nobody ever saw him get into the water), set out to design a pier which would be perfect for swimmers to enjoy. The pier legs were designed in such a way that swimmers would be able to climb up them and jump off. The diving platform at the end of the pier could be reached via a set of steps.

Swimmers would be able to launch themselves into the depths of the Bristol Channel from a great height.

The pier was opened to much fanfare in 1869. The first person to swim around the end of the pier was the designer himself. At least, he claimed he was, although he swam around it before anyone else got up, There were no witnesses. He would often be seen at the beach at high tide chatting with locals and telling them that he had been in already. Hans passed on his love of swimming to his children and grandchildren. One of his descendants still swims at the pier to this day.

Unfortunately, commercial interests soon took over and the future of swims around the end of the pier was placed in jeopardy. There was no money to be made from swimmers unless they visited one of the seafront cafes after their swim. Instead, the pier company decided that the pier would be a great launch point for boat trips in the channel. Great ships like the Waverly and Balmoral would dock at the end of the pier, allowing passengers to get on board. Disgracefully, the steps which had been designed to allow access to the diving platform were shut off to swimmers. Fines were issued to any rebels who dared to climb the steps and dive off the end of the pier. There were mixed feelings about this amongst locals. Hans Price was said to be absolutely furious that his pier was not being used for the purpose it was designed for.

Swimmers continued to swim around the end of the pier, although they were banned from doing so on days when the steamer boats were present. At 310 metres long, it provided a real challenge for swimmers who had to correctly judge the currents or risk being swept away to Weston. There are a number of recorded instances of this happening. One swimmer, Bert Bradford, swam around the pier an incredible two hours after high tide. He was swept down to Middle Hope and had to walk back to Clevedon in his trunks.

Another hazard for swimmers came when a decision was taken by the pier management to allow anglers to fish from the pier. The necessity to avoid the fishing lines made the swim around the end of the pier even more treacherous. Again, Hans Price was very angry. Sadly, he had no power to challenge the decision. The pier, which had been designed by a swimmer for the benefit of swimmers, had become a commercial enterprise and the needs of swimmers were no longer taken into account.

Swimmers continued to swim from the pier beach though. One of the most famous moments in Clevedon history came in 1873 when Mildred Summerhayes swam under the pier on the first ever Ladye Bay swim. Sadly, Mildred died just after her swim but her example encouraged many others and the pier beach was soon opened up to women bathers as well as men.

Swimming continued to be popular in the 20th century. Gertrude Higginbottom wrote about her experiences.

"In my youth I would often swim around the pier when tide times allowed. I first attempted a swim around the pier at the age of 11. Unfortunately, I slightly misjudged the tide times and the currents swept me under the pier before I got to the end. I was able to swim safely back to shore but I felt extremely disappointed. Even at such a young age, I was well aware of the dangers posed by the Bristol Channel. My parents had always told me to respect the sea and, thankfully, I was sensible enough to listen to their warnings. I had to wait until the following summer to complete the swim. I felt an enormous sense of pride as I rounded the end of the pier. I saw the steps which led to the diving platform and I wished that I could have climbed them and dived into the sea. Sadly, security guards were present and, even if they hadn't been, they had recently installed CCTV cameras so any wrong doing on my part would have been captured on camera and I would have been prosecuted. Diving from the pier legs continued. This activity was frowned upon by pier management but there was not much which could be done to prevent it. I remember being shouted at to get down by pier staff on a number of occasions. Of course, I did as they requested and launched myself into the water. It was great fun.

Diving from the pier became very popular in the 1960s. Led by a charismatic character named Frederick Tebay, who I had known for many years, swimmers would swim to the pier legs, climb up and then jump or dive into the water. I was normally on lengthy training swims so I rarely participated, but I did witness Freddie's diving on several occasions. He had some rather interesting ways of entering the water and hundreds of people would gather on the beach to enjoy his performance.

Then, one day, in 1969, disaster struck. Tebay led a group to the pier. I was there that day and I witnessed events from within the water. There must have been close to twenty of them climbing the pier and I remember feeling concerned that the pier may not take their combined weight. I regret not intervening, although I don't think they would have listened to me anyway. My worst fears were confirmed when the pier leg collapsed into the water. Without the leg to support the rest of the structure, a whole section of the pier collapsed soon after. Tebay and his gang miraculously escaped unscathed but the damage to the pier was done

Little was done to try and repair the pier. Her broken body stood there as a sad reminder of her glorious past. It was expected that she would eventually collapse into the sea. However, one fateful day in 1979 would revive her fortunes and lead to her eventual re-opening.

When The Queen visited Clevedon and completed the famous Ladye Bay swim with me, she was shocked to see the sad state of disrepair the pier had fallen into. She insisted that she must be restored. From that day onwards, I dedicated much of my life towards getting the pier reopened. It took a lot of work and a lot of fundraising but, in 1989, our work was rewarded and the pier was fully restored to her former glory. I was honoured to be asked to officially reopen the pier after the Queen turned down her invitation as she was busy shooting animals at Balmoral.

A wonderful party was held that day. Fifteen minutes before high tide, a group of swimmers, led by myself and Gavin Price (representing his three-time great grandfather), swam around the end of the pier. For one day only, the steps at the end of the pier were opened up to swimmers and we were allowed to climb up to the diving platform where we all jumped into the water. It was one of the happiest days of my life".

The pier continues to stand proud to this day and, hopefully, will do so for centuries to come.

FREDERICK TEBAY- THE PEOPLE'S CHAMPION

Frederick Tebay is remembered by most as the man who broke Clevedon Pier in 1969. However, he was a very famous diver in his youth and even competed in the Olympic Games.

Born in Yatton in 1908, Tebay grew up swimming in the marine lake. He was a member of Clevedon swimming club, but he was never going to be a champion swimmer. His life changed when a pontoon was added to the marine lake in 1919. There was much excitement at the addition of the new pontoon, not least because it was to be opened by His Majesty, King George V. The opening of the pontoon attracted tens of thousands of people to the lake, all excited to see the King,

Gertrude Higginbottom recalls the events surrounding the King's visit.

"We were all very excited when we heard that the King was coming to Clevedon. We were even more excited about the new pontoon. I think the whole of Clevedon was there that day. The pontoon could only be reached by water so a boat was provided to transport His Majesty across for the unveiling. His Majesty, however, refused the offer of a boat ride and announced that he would swim to the pontoon instead. The crowd went wild. Fortunately, the King had brought his swimming costume along. He tentatively got into the lake and set off on the fifty metres swim to the pontoon.

He swam heads up breaststroke, giving us no idea of his true swimming ability. The boat accompanied him in case of emergency, but he was never going to need it. Arriving at the pontoon, he climbed up to unveil the plaque.

"I now declare this pontoon open", he proudly announced. " May all who jump and dive from her be kept safe from harm. In the Glory of God. Amen". He then dived into the lake to an almighty roar from the crowd, before showing off his best front crawl to swim back to the steps. We were very impressed.

Once His Majesty had got dressed and faffed for about an hour, he headed up to the Salthouse for a private function. My mother and father were on the guest list but us kids were not invited. Not that we cared. We were desperate to try out the new pontoon. As many as one hundred children set out on the swim for the pontoon. One after another, we climbed out and jumped or dived into the lake. We absolutely loved it".

One of those children is believed to have been Frederick Tebay. Over the next few years, he spent all of his free time on that pontoon. He became addicted to diving into the lake and it wasn't long before he quit the swimming club. As he became better and better, he needed a new challenge. Keen to support their son, his parents campaigned for a diving board to be added to the lake, which, in due course, it was. The diving board was several metres high and provided a much sterner test for Tebay. Not long after, a springboard followed.

Tebay spent hundreds of hours perfecting his technique over the next few years. He developed his own dives and attracted huge crowds to the lake. At the tender age of 19. He was selected to represent Great Britain at the Amsterdam Olympics of 1928. He was looking forward to attending the games with his best friend Johnny, although he wasn't looking forward to rooming with him. Sadly, the

IOC barred Johnny from competing at the last minute, meaning that Tebay had to travel out on his own.

Tebay put on a diving masterclass in Amsterdam. The Dutch fans went absolutely berserk every time he climbed to the top of the board. For many, his diving was the highlight of the entire games. Sadly, for Tebay, the judges did not share the crowd's enthusiasm. Tebay's unconventional approach did not win their favour and he failed to reach the final. The stands erupted in displeasure at the judge's decision and there was a mini riot. They were shouting out Tebay's name and demanding that he be reinstated into the competition. The judges, though, stood firm in their decision and Tebay was sent home.

Tebay returned to Clevedon a hero. Thousands turned up for his arrival at Bristol Airport and an open top bus tour was held in Clevedon to celebrate his achievements. Despite returning home without a medal, he was considered to be the People's Champion. It is doubtful that he would have got a better reception if he had returned home with gold.

Sadly, that was to be the end of Tebay's competitive international diving career. The Great Britain selectors told him he needed to adapt his technique if he wished to be selected again, but he refused. This was not a bad move on Tebay's part. The Olympics had turned him into a global celebrity and he spent the next ten years touring the world, putting on exhibition events. There was barely a major global city where he did not put on one of his shows and Tebay became a very rich man. He did not forget his routes, though, and returned to Clevedon every year to put on a free show at the lake. The whole of Clevedon would turn out to watch plus many thousands more.

The war put a stop to Tebay's diving career. He was 30 when the war began and was sent to fight in Europe. Thankfully, he survived the war but decided not to resume his diving career afterwards. He hadn't had any time to practice his diving in the preceding six years and he felt unable to rediscover his former glories. Of course, he continued to dive for fun in Clevedon and spent many years coaching local children how to dive. He was still diving in 1969 when he caused the collapse of the pier. Tebay was so mortified at what he had done that he never dived again. He died in Clevedon in 1988 and his ashes were scattered in the marine lake.

Tebay's grandson, Paul, continues to dive in Clevedon. He has inherited much of his grandfather's eccentricity, if not his ability. Sadly, for Paul, the diving boards at the lake are long gone due to namby-pamby health and safety regulations. However, the pontoon remains and Paul continues to perform a number of his grandfather's dives to this very day.

DOGS IN CLEVEDON

As we all know, dogs are banned from both the lake and the pier beach in Clevedon. There have been many challenges to these rules over the years, sometimes from some very notable people.

The most famous example came from no less than Her Majesty, Queen Elizabeth II. When she completed her Ladye Bay swim in 1979, her corgis ran on to the beach to greet her. This was met by much disgust from locals although, unsurprisingly, nobody had the temerity to challenge her.

The imposition of the dog ban goes back much further though. Coleridge wrote in his diary in the late 18th century about the ban on dogs at the lake.

"One enjoys a morning stroll from my abode, across the Poets' Walk and back down to the lake. My loyal border collie, Misty, always accompanies me. No dog enjoys a swim more than Misty and I consider the ban on dogs swimming in the lake to be extremely unjust. High tide rarely coincides with my morning stroll so Misty often misses out on her swim. Thankfully, the lake was deserted on our arrival this morning and Misty and I were able to enjoy a wondrous dip as the sun rose. We felt we had won a victory over the petty rule makers".

Locals were not happy with Coleridge. Mr. William Pennyfarthing wrote to the Woodspring Chronicle to express his disgust.

"Mr Coleridge is a visitor to this town. World famous poet he may well be but the rules apply to him as much as they do to the next man. I am mindful to take my shotgun to the lake on future visits. If I see Misty in the lake again, Mr Coleridge should expect his loyal friend to receive a bullet".

Thankfully, such extreme action was never resorted to, but Coleridge was driven out of town by his refusal to follow the rules. He may have spent the rest of his life in Clevedon otherwise. We will never know.

"With a heavy heart, myself and Misty left Clevedon forever today. The locals have taken exception to Misty and her love for swimming and we no longer feel safe here. Threats against her life have been made and we have both received abuse on our morning stroll. This is no way to exist and we shall find somewhere more friendly and welcoming to live".

As Clevedon became a popular tourist town in the Victorian era, the lake became more and more crowded in the summer months. As the crowds got bigger, dogs became more and more of a problem.

The brother of the pier designer Hans Price, a Mr. Stefan Price, set himself up as an official dog warden at the lake. Any dog walkers would be politely asked to leave and to take their mutts with them. If they refused then Price would try to take their dogs away from them. Sometimes he would succeed and he would take the dogs to a local pound to be humanely destroyed. Price had no concern for the dogs, which he revealed in an interview with the Tickenham Ticker.

"Dogs have no place at our lake. They are filthy creatures who carry disease and bite children. I take great pleasure in having them destroyed. Dog owners are free to take their smelly beasts to Little Harp beach or up to Poets' Walk.

Please do not bring them to the lake or they shall be dealt with harshly".

The dog problem remains the same today, although dogs are no longer destroyed if they visit the lake. Price's four-time great nephew, Gavin, continued the family tradition for some time and chased dogs away if they dared to stray into the lake or its surrounds.

BETTY THE RECORD BREAKER

Not all dogs in Clevedon have been a pest. One dog became famous in 1932 when she became the first to complete the Ladye Bay swim. Betty (named after Betty of Betty and Mildred fame), was a cocker spaniel who often swam in the sea at Ladye Bay with her owner, a Mrs. Roberts (first name unknown). Mrs. Roberts, an eccentric, elderly Welsh widow, lived alone in a huge house on Dial Hill. Gertrude Higginbottom tells the story of Betty's first Ladye Bay swim.

"As children, we were rather afraid of Mrs. Roberts. We would often see her swimming at Ladye Bay but we kept well away from her. She had never had children of her own and did not seem to be a fan of us youngsters. However, when she got Betty, she seemed to mellow somewhat. The children loved to play with Betty and Mrs. Roberts was happy as long as her beloved mutt was happy. Mrs. Roberts swam at Ladye Bay most days with Betty but they never ventured far from shore.

One day, I was approaching the final leg of a twelve-way Ladye Bay swim when I saw Mrs. Roberts and Betty get into the water. They did this every day but, this time, things felt different. I had never seen Betty swim with a tow float before, but she was using one today, as was Mrs. Roberts. They seemed to be setting off with some purpose as they passed me going the other way. A couple of minutes later, I made it to Ladye Bay and turned around to head back to the pier. As I turned, I could see two tow floats bobbing up and down in the waves in the distance. I gradually closed the gap and I passed them just before the pier. Betty seemed to be really enjoying herself and I felt excited that I was about to see history being made.

As I reached the slipway, I got out of the water and turned around to see how the potential record breaker was getting on. Betty was about 50 metres behind me alongside Mrs. Roberts. Then, out of nowhere, a baying mob of locals ran down the slipway shouting abuse at Betty and Mrs. Roberts (first name unknown).

"Get that frigging dog away from our beach" screamed out one man. Except he didn't say frigging, he used another word beginning with f. More abuse followed, none of it suitable to go to print.

As Betty struggled to get up onto the slipway, she was pushed back into the water by the angry mob. One more time she struggled to get out but, this time, one especially nasty local picked her up and flung her downstream into the strongest part of the current. She was swept away and Mrs. Roberts, not surprisingly, set off after her, after giving the mob a bit of abuse of her own. Eventually, they reached the beach by the bandstand (where dogs are not banned) and they were able to get out of the water unopposed. Betty was cold and tired but she had treats and water in her tow float and she soon perked up.

Sadly, Betty did not make it into the Guinness Book of Records. Ross McWhirter said the swim could not be recognised as Betty did not get out at the pier beach. Mrs. Roberts said this decision was ridiculous as Betty had actually swum farther than the required distance. McWhirter, though, refused to back down. He argued that the guidelines were clear, swimmers must enter the water at Ladye Bay and get out at the pier beach. The swimmer must get out on the pebbles, the slipway did not count as it was a man-made feature.

Mrs. Roberts was not going to take this lying down. She took the McWhirter brothers to court, demanding that Betty should be included in the book. The judge was sympathetic, summarising that, in his opinion, Betty had completed the swim. However, the McWhirter brothers had founded the Guinness Book of Records and were free to set their own rules for their own book. Mrs. Roberts lost the case.

The court case destroyed Mrs. Robers financially and she was forced to sell her big house. She moved into a tiny studio flat close to Aldi and she was never the same again. She died in 1935, a broken woman. Betty survived another three years but she never got over the passing of her owner. She was buried alongside Mrs. Roberts (first name unknown) in the graveyard of St. Andrew's Church.

The story took an unexpected twist when the McWhirter brothers visited Clevedon in 1977 to witness Jack McDonald's record attempt. They expressed regret for not ratifying Betty's swim as a record breaker and unveiled a plaque on the beach by the bandstand in recognition of her achievement. Betty's swim has been recorded in all subsequent editions of the Guinness Book of Records.

To this day, Betty remains the only dog to have completed this swim".

Some years later, Gertrude came across the grave of Mrs. Roberts on a post-swim stroll around Poets' Walk. She was immensely saddened to see the terrible state it was in and felt an enormous amount of guilt that she hadn't done more to support Mrs. Roberts when she was alive. She wrote this heartfelt poem that same day.

Mrs. Roberts

To dear Mrs. Roberts, your first name unknown
An untended grave with the weeds overgrown
In life overlooked, for the most part forlorn
Then when you departed, few bothered to mourn
But, despite this you felt such a pride in your town
With your loyal friend Betty, you swam all the way down
Ladye Bay to the bandstand, swept well past the pier
But, Norris and Ross, they would make it so clear
No record for Betty, no place in the sun
All your dreams of salvation, so cruelly undone
A terrible ending for two friends, so damn brave
Now abandoned, forgotten, in that overgrown grave.

THE CLEVEDON MAFIA

We all know Clevedon as a peaceful, friendly town and many people probably think it has always been that way. It will come as a shock to many that, in the 1930s, Clevedon was run by the mafia and the town was subjected to a reign of terror.

Francesco's was a popular seafront cafe in Clevedon during much of the 1930s in the building which now houses Tiffin. The cafe was massively popular with day trippers, locals and sea swimmers. However, not everything was as it seemed.

Francesco was a keen swimmer. He had represented Italy in international competition in his younger days. He moved to England in 1932 with the idea of setting up a cafe to act as a front for his main business. Francesco was a failed mafia man in Italy. He could not get his own patch and he saw Clevedon as a great place due to her popularity with wild swimmers. Not only could Francesco swim every day in Clevedon, but he would be able to rule over the swimming community with a rod of steel.

Gertrude lived through the Francesco years.

"When Francesco first came to Clevedon, we thought he was just a friendly cafe owner. We all enjoyed his food and we would often use his cafe for a cuppa and a slice of cake after our sea swims. However, we soon learnt that Francesco was not as friendly as we first thought. He declared that all swimming gear must be purchased from him. We could not even keep any of our old gear. His family would patrol the beaches and the lake. Any old gear would be confiscated and destroyed. We would then need to purchase brand new items from Francesco. We weren't happy but we couldn't swim without our masses of swim kit so we had no choice.

Clevedon had always been a peaceful town so the presence of Francesco and his family came as something of a shock. They took over the swimming shop on Hill Road and immediately put up all prices by fifty percent. We had no alternative but to shop there. I lost all my treasured swimming gear overnight and had to replace it all at Francesco's inflated prices. I could barely afford to do this, but I was rather fond of my knees and I wanted to keep them.

I remember one occasion when a young girl turned up at the lake in a Charlie McLeod. Francesco was furious. He had an exclusive deal with Dryrobe and there was no chance he would stand for this. Francesco put his friendly persona into play and spoke to the little girl to find out where she had got her robe. She proudly announced that her Mummy and Daddy had given it to her for her birthday. Later that day, on his way home from work, the little girl's father was knocked off of his bike and brutally kneecapped. The police refused to get involved".

There was very little dissent against Francesco, at least not in public. However, one local, a Mr. Alfred Williams did write to the Clevedon Mercury to express his opposition.

"Francesco has no power over me. I will not do as he says. I have had my dryrobe for twenty years and I shall be wearing it for another twenty. He can piss right off".

That night, the offices of the Clevedon Mercury were burnt to the ground. Mr. Williams mysteriously disappeared and was never seen again.

Swimmers were not the only people who had to fear the new mafia. Francesco was not a fan of dogs and he was very keen to enforce the dog ban at the lake and pier beach. Francesco's sons would patrol the beach and lake throughout the day, shotguns at the ready. Any dog which dared stray into banned territory would be shot on sight. Thankfully for the dogs, none ever received a bullet. Local dog owners were, rightfully, terrified of Francesco and nobody dared to take their dog even close to the lake.

Francesco was not all bad though. He set up a casino at the end of the pier and the locals loved going there to try and win some money. Gertrude reminisces.

"One time, my brother, Cedric, played in a poker tournament at the end of the pier. The opposition included a couple of Francesco's sons. Cedric loved his poker and it was no surprise to us that he won the tournament and pocketed a healthy four figure sum (which was a lot of money in those days). We all thought Francesco would be furious, but far from it. He celebrated with Cedric and bought him drinks to show there were no hard feelings. Unfortunately for Cedric, he didn't handle his drink very well. He got very drunk and, somehow, he fell off the pier on the walk back home. He was able to swim back to shore but there was no sign of his cash in his pockets when he got out of the water. We can only assume that it got washed away by the sea. Francesco expressed his sympathy but, regretfully, he said there was nothing he could do about the missing cash. Cedric was not the only person to fall off the pier after a big victory. Heavy drinking and Clevedon Pier did not seem to be a great combination.

The 1930s were not happy times in Clevedon due to Francesco's reign of terror. My father was the only person brave enough to stand up to him. He told Francesco that he was a guest in our town and he should show us more respect. Francesco was not happy, but he did like my father and he did not want to kneecap him. Instead, he offered my father a deal. His son, Lanfranco would take on my brother, Bert, in a boxing match on the pontoon. The loser's family would have to leave Clevedon forever.

Bert was a good boxer at regional level, but Lanfranco was one of the up-and-coming stars in the sport. He was even being talked of as a future world champion. We all knew Bert had very little chance and we had already packed our bags before the fight took place. We planned to move to Weston-Super-Mare and start new lives there. To make matters worse, Francesco and his other sons were the judges for the fight. Bert's only hope was a knock-out,

Bert did not lack confidence, but even he knew he had little chance. The lake was packed that day. My Uncle Neville, never one to turn down a business opportunity, decided to act as bookmaker for the fight. Francesco placed a massive bet on Lanfranco. Neville did not have enough money to pay him out but he could not turn down the bet. Like us, he was praying for a miracle.

The fight went as expected. Lanfranco dominated and was well ahead going into the final round. Even with neutral judges, Bert would have had no chance of a points victory. Bert was clinging on for dear life and we were all proud of his effort. Going into the last minute the game was up though. Lanfranco had him on the ropes and Bert was struggling to stay on his feet. He had done the Higginbottoms proud, but it was not enough. Then, something unexpected happened. I didn't notice at first but a young boy in the crowd shouted out behind me,

"Lanfranco's shoelace has come undone".

It wasn't long before everyone had noticed. Everyone except Lanfranco. Unaware that he was facing imminent disaster, Lanfranco kept boxing away. There were twenty seconds left on the clock when Lanfranco tripped on his laces. Unbalanced, Bert seized his opportunity and landed a perfect uppercut on the Italian. Lanfranco flew through the ropes and landed in the lake. The strength of Bert's punch had rendered Lanfranco unconscious. Thankfully, a lifeguard was on duty and he was rescued.

The crowd went absolutely wild. Francesco's reign of terror was over. He may have been battered and bruised but Bert was a hero. Uncle Neville breathed a sigh of relief as did the whole of the Higginbottom clan. We were staying in Clevedon.

Say what you want about Francesco but he was a man of his word. The next morning, all sign of him was gone. We never heard of him again and Clevedon was, once again, a peaceful place".

THE MONKS' TRUNKS

By the 1930s, the Clevedon friars were only swimming down from Ladye Bay once a week, from the start of April to the end of October. They continued to swim naked as the discomfort this made them feel was considered an essential part of their sacrifice to atone for their sins. Francesco sensed a business opportunity due to his growing trade in selling swimwear and swim equipment to the people of Clevedon.

Francesco was a devout Catholic and attended services at the Church of the Immaculate Conception several times a week. When the Superior General of the Church refused his request to supply the friars with swimming costumes, he was not sure what to do. Even Francesco was not going to start kneecapping a man of God.

Francesco opted to search for a more suitable solution. He contacted the Vatican to seek clarification on whether or not it was essential that the friars swam naked. He was invited to the Vatican for a meeting with the Pope. The Pope told Francesco that, yes, it was indeed considered important that the friars swam naked. However, he liked Francesco and wanted to support his growing business in Clevedon. He told Francesco that if he could design a costume which was even more unsightly and humiliating for the friars than swimming naked, he was willing to consider it.

Francesco came from Milan and he had many contacts in the leading Milan fashion houses. In no time at all, he had designers hard at work. Designs were completed in a matter of weeks and Francesco was summoned back to the Vatican to show the Pope the prototype.

To Francesco's relief, the Pope was delighted with the designs. He even ordered a couple of pairs for himself. Francesco returned to Clevedon a happy man. The friars were, initially, delighted that they would no longer have to swim naked. However, their mood changed when they saw what they would actually be wearing. The order had come from the Pope though, so they had no choice but to comply and wear the new trunks.

Francesco could not predict how popular these new trunks would become. It was not long before the new 'Monks' Trunks', as they became known, were selling far and wide. Francesco recruited leading Hollywood celebrities to model the trunks in advertising campaigns which went global. He became a very rich man.

Francesco was no idiot. He never wore the new trunks himself, at least not in public. He knew how awful they looked. Regrettably, the Monks' Trunks are every bit as popular today. They are more commonly referred to as 'budgie smugglers' and they look just as awful now as they did ninety years ago. Next time you see an overweight man squeezing into these hideous trunks, remind yourself of the fascinating history which led to their creation.

FINS AND FLIPPERS

Gertrude remembers another of Mr. Bartholomew's inventions.

"Mr. Batholomew is best known as the man who invented the yo-yo, but he also invented what we now know as 'fins' and 'flippers'. I always called them 'cheat feet'.

Mr. Bartholomew first came up with the designs in 1925 when I was 13 years old. He designed them as a swimming aid. We all got to try them out and it was noticeable how much faster they made us swim. I was always the fastest swimmer in our group, but it wasn't long before some of my friends were able to beat me because of the fins they were wearing on their feet. Although I had tried them out, my father told me that I would not wear them again. "You don't need to cheat Gertie", he told me. "Your friends may be beating you. but at what cost to their dignity?". I knew my father was right. I would let them have their moment of glory, but they would have to live with the guilt of their dishonest actions for the rest of their lives.

My Uncle Neville, however, was not bothered about such things. He saw the potential of the 'cheat feet' and he teamed up with Mr. Bartholomew to market and sell them. Not surprisingly, they were very successful and it wasn't long before they were a common sight in Clevedon, Weston-Super-Mare and in public pools throughout the west country. When Mr. Bartholomew died suddenly, my Uncle Neville continued to market and sell them with Mrs. Bartholomew as a silent partner. This time, my Uncle Neville thought he had cracked it. He was going to be rich.

Sadly, everything changed when the mafia came to Clevedon. My uncle was banned from selling the 'cheat feet' immediately and Francesco took control. Francesco confiscated all the 'cheat feet' which were already in circulation and destroyed them. A keen swimmer himself, he did not approve of them as, like me and my father, he considered their use to be a form of cheating. He banned 'cheat feet' from being used with immediate effect and they disappeared from Clevedon.

When the mafia were chased out of Clevedon, 'cheat feet' returned, but my Uncle Neville was not able to take advantage. Mr. Bartholomew, rather stupidly, had not patented his design and they were now in production all over the country. Just like with the yo-yo, Mr. Batholomew's family were not able to enjoy the riches which his design should have brought them. My Uncle Neville, as always, dusted himself down and moved on to search for the next business opportunity".

I wrote this poem about these new inventions.

Cheat Feet

What's going on with all these cheat feet?
You swim with fins but others know
That when you wear those silly cheat feet
You're out to cheat because you're slow
I didn't know you swam in cheat feet
I thought you'd won, I felt depressed
But when I saw you in your cheat feet
I knew you'd cheated, I'm not impressed
So, when I see you're in your cheat feet
I have mixed feelings, I must admit
Cos even when you're wearing cheat feet
You won but only by a bit
So, have some guts and ditch those cheat feet
We'll race as equals, it's only fair

And then you'll see, without your cheat feet
That I will beat you fair and square.

THE CLEVEDON 'OLYMPICS'

When the IOC refused outdoor swimming's application to be an Olympic sport in 1931, the WWSA (World Wild Swimming Association) refused to take the decision lying down. There was much excitement when they announced that a world-championships of wild swimming would take place. There was a lot of competition to stage the inaugural event which was set to be staged in the summer of 1933. Clevedon, not surprisingly, chose to make a bid. Given the fame achieved by Johnny Guffington and Frederick Tebay, not to mention the wonderful sea and lake swimming which Clevedon provides, the decision was always going to be a formality. Clevedon was awarded the Games with almost unanimous support.

The town had never staged an event on this scale before. Hundreds of athletes would be travelling to Clevedon from all corners of the world, although, with air travel still in its infancy, most would be travelling from western Europe. The whole of Clevedon was firmly behind the event. Many households hosted an athlete for the duration of the Games, although some of the bigger stars opted to stay in the Walton Park Hotel. Hundreds of locals chose to volunteer to help run the event.

When King George V officially opened the Games on the 15th of August 1933, the whole town was bursting with pride. There was a real carnival atmosphere. For the first time ever, the eyes of the world were on Clevedon.

The Games opened in style with what would turn out to be the first ever Long Swim, although the official records do not list it as such. There was much hope of a local victory through Johnny Guffington and Gertrude Higginbottom was thought to have an outside chance of a medal.

However, it was a disappointing day for local fans. Gertrude finished a respectable sixth in the women's race but the distance was always going to be too short to play to her strengths.

Guffington's failure was more of a disappointment. The WWSA, unlike the IOC, had not banned Guffington's signature move. THE WWSA knew that Guffington's participation was essential for the event to be a success, as he was so popular in the town. There were complaints from other nations but their protests fell on deaf ears. Guffington, donning his new pair of 'Monks' Trunks', was well down in 10th place as he approached the pier. At this point, his bottom let out an almighty roar and he flew into a clear lead. The winner was to be the first swimmer to get out at the slipway. Unfortunately, Johnny's fart propelled him well past the slipway and towards the sailing club. By the time he had turned around and swum back to the slipway, he had finished in a disappointing 18th place. The home crowd's mood was not helped by both races being won by French swimmers. The medal ceremonies were conducted in near silence.

With the Ladye Bay swim complete, attention turned to the lake. Frederick Tebay, not surprisingly, chose to come out of retirement for his home event. He was going for quadruple gold in the high board, springboard, pontoon and the spectacular pier end which was due to be the highlight of the diving competition. The high board was the first to take place.

Tebay was up against the Italian diving superstar, Fernando Ferrari. With Tebay only participating in exhibition events, Ferrari was dominant in world diving. This would be their first and only meeting as Tebay had already announced that this would be his final competitive event. Most pundits believed that Tebay did enough to take gold in the high board, but, controversially, Ferrari took the spoils, with Tebay in second. Many believe that the judges were threatened by the Clevedon mafia who were running the town at the time. We will never know if the result was fixed but then, for no apparent reason, Tebay withdrew from all remaining events. It is believed that his family would be in danger if he continued to compete. It was a very sad way for his diving career to end. Ferrari ended up with four golds but they were hollow victories and he was greeted by loud boos every time he dived. Even Francesco and his family could not force the local crowd to get behind Ferrari.

The lake held many swimming races. Guffington dominated the men's events, farting his way to six gold medals. His Ladye Bay failure was soon forgotten by the crowd. Sadly, in an unconnected event, many swimmers became ill after swimming in the lake. It is not known why but many accused Guffington of dirtying the water. Of course, they were rightly dismissed as bad losers.

The final event was to be a swim from Portishead to Clevedon. This was the one everyone had been looking forward to. Competitors would enter from the slipway on Sugar Loaf beach in Portishead and swim, under Clevedon Pier, to get out of the water at the slipway on pier beach. Tens of thousands watched from the coast path.

The men set off as the tide turned with the women setting off half an hour later. Again, Guffington messed up his tactics and overshot the finish. This time, the field was much more spread out and he had time to swim back and claim the bronze medal. He knew though that it should have been gold. Guffington was a fierce competitor and, it is believed, he was far more focused on the two that got away than the six golds which he had actually won.

The home crowd, though, were more interested in the women's race. This was the big chance for Gertrude HIgginbottom to take a medal over a distance which played far more to her strengths. The race looked likely to be a match between Higginbottom and the Swedish superstar, Annika Larsson. Larsson and Higginbottom were good friends but today, they were rivals.

I'll let Gertrude tell us the story of the race.

"As expected, the start of the race was very fast. Everyone was fighting for position. I am a notoriously slow starter and found myself down in midfield and boxed in. I knew it was a long swim to the finish, though, and I had plenty of time to make ground. Unfortunately, for me, Annika was a strong starter and I faced an almighty battle to catch her. By the time we reached Black Nore Lighthouse, the field was beginning to string out and I had plenty of room to overtake. Larsson had a big lead already but I had worked my way up to fifth place. I used the swimmers in front of me as targets and I picked them off, one by one. By the time we reached Charlcombe Bay, I had passed everyone but Larsson. I could see her tow float in the distance but she had a big lead. I was not about to give up, but I knew my chances of catching her were slim.

From Charlcombe Bay, the current really picks up. There may have been two and a half miles to swim, but it would only take us about half an hour. I was going to have to get a move on if I was going to catch her. Slowly but surely, I could see her tow float in the distance getting closer and closer, but I was running out of time. As we were swept past Ladye Bay, she had about a fifty metre lead. I was not closing fast enough but I had one factor in my favour. I knew these currents better than anyone but Larsson had only swum here a couple of times before. My local knowledge was going to be a big plus. As we passed the hotel, Larsson swam further out than me and swam right into an eddy. This was my big chance. I nipped up her inside and halved the gap in no time at all. She was soon through the eddy but I could sense she was beginning to tire. The gap closed to twenty metres, then fifteen, then ten. Again, I found a faster current than her. As we were swept under the pier, I pulled alongside her. It was now a straight fight to the slipway.

Neither of us had any strength left for a sprint finish. It was now a battle of survival. Thankfully, I had trained for distances far longer than this, whereas Larsson was at her limit. Inch by inch, I started pulling away from her. Even with my earplugs in, I could hear the roar from the stands. Inches turned to a foot, then two feet, then a yard. As I reached the slipway, I had two yards in hand. Two yards after four and a half miles! I got out on the slipway to be greeted by a wall of sound. I had done it. I was the world champion!

It was a proud moment when the Prime Minister, Ramsey McDonald, presented me with my medal. I was even prouder when I found out that the BBC's live broadcast of the event had attracted record viewing figures. All those millions of people tuning in just to watch me. I couldn't believe it".

Gertrude's gold was the last act of a wonderful games which had firmly put Clevedon on the map. There was much excitement in the town at what the future could hold. Mrs. Freda Tunnock wrote to the Clevedon Herald.

"Clevedon has really made a name for herself over the last week. Our hosting of these Championships has been exemplary. We have proven our ability to put on these massive events. Surely, it has to be the Olympics next or, at the very least, the Empire Games".

However, Paul Hardington wrote an article in the Kenn Explorer disagreeing.

"Clevedon does not have the infrastructure to host an Olympic Games. Traffic is already bad enough during rush hour in the town centre. We lack even the most basic facilities and we do not have the hotel rooms. Hosting the Olympics would bankrupt the town".

Despite the opposition, Clevedon put in a serious bid to host the 1948 Olympics. It was a very close call as to whether London or Clevedon would be put forward as Great Britain's candidate for host city. London won by one vote and went on to be selected by the IOC to host the games. Not many realise how close Clevedon came to hosting the 1948 Olympics.

The growth of the Olympic Games means that Clevedon is not big enough to host such an event these days. There was talk of a joint bid with Portishead for the 2012 Games but it was decided that London had better credentials and the bid never really got off the ground. Sadly, it seems that Clevedon will never again host an event on the scale of those 1933 World Championships.

BUCKETS AND SPADES

Gertrude remembers her Uncle Neville and a very successful business venture.

"Clevedon was massively popular with day trippers in the 1920s and 1930s. With the railways still running to Clevedon and foreign holidays still a distant dream, crowds would flock to Clevedon in their thousands. There wasn't space to swing a cat on the seafront and business in the town was thriving.

The one thing Clevedon lacked was an easily accessible sandy beach. As a result, the bucket and spade shop on Hill Road was doing no trade. In 1928, the owners gave up and shut the shop down.

My Uncle Neville was a shrewd businessman and he saw an opportunity. He bought up all their unused stock at rock bottom prices. We all wondered what he was going to do with these buckets and spades. My guess was that he had a contact in Weston-Super-Mare and he would sell them on at a profit. Uncle Neville had other plans.

The large sandbank which runs down from the pier past the lake, about a quarter of a mile off shore, was a vast, unspoilt area which Uncle Neville was ready to exploit. That said, it was hardly ideal. It wasn't exposed for more than a couple of hours at high tide and, on neap tides, it wasn't exposed at all. With the hassle of getting out there and back in again, the time it was available would be reduced further. However, the site had one big advantage. As the sandbank was below the high-water mark, any business done there would not be subject to UK taxation laws. Uncle Neville knew that this opportunity would have a limited lifespan, but the novelty value, alone, would generate a lot of interest in the short term. He had to get in fast before others had the same idea.

In the summer of 1929, my uncle set up a stall on the sandbank selling buckets and spades. With a loud halo to attract business from the shoreline, he soon had excited children dragging their parents across to the sandbank. There they would purchase a bucket and spade each and set about playing in the sand before the tide came back in. Uncle Neville was no mug and he knew the parents would soon get bored watching the children playing in the sand. First, he set up a deckchair hire business, then, in 1930, he set up a small cafe. Due to the logistical difficulties of taking everything out to the sandbank and back in again before the tide came in, he only sold tea and Victoria sponge. These were simple times though and this was more than enough to keep parents happy, whilst their children made sandcastles.

As the tide turned, Uncle Neville would blow a whistle to give visitors a fifteen-minute warning to get back to the beach. Of course, once the children had purchased their buckets and spades, they would want to come back time and time again. Uncle Neville had to buy more deckchairs and he even hired an assistant to run the cafe. Business was thriving but, sadly, it wouldn't last.

One day in 1935, business was especially brisk. The cafe assistant had phoned in sick and Uncle Neville was run off his feet trying to keep his customers happy. He was so busy that he lost track of the time and forgot to blow his whistle to warn everyone that the tide was coming in. There were over two hundred people on that sandbank that day and they were all trapped by the incoming tide. Lifeboats were employed from Portishead, Weston-Super-Mare and Burnham-on-Sea and they rescued many people. Many others were strong swimmers and got back into shore safely, but not all were saved. Tragically, eleven people drowned and the council took the controversial decision to suspend Uncle Neville from trading.

My uncle was distraught at what had happened. He sold all of his remaining buckets and spades to a trader in Weston-Super-Mare and he never ran his own business again. He never talked about what happened that day.

I've often wondered if there was the potential to run another business from that sandbank. However, these days, the namby-pamby liberal left would probably put a stop to it before you could even get started. It's very rare you will see a bucket and spade in Clevedon these days but, whenever I do, I'm always reminded of my Uncle Neville and the wonderful times we enjoyed on that sandbank".

PISSY CORNER

Many of us have made use of the facilities at Pissy Corner, on pier beach, when caught short after a sea swim. Not many of us will be aware, though, of the fascinating history behind this place.

The first documented evidence of the existence of Pissy Corner comes from a poem by the great Alfred Lord Tennyson. Tennyson is known to have visited Clevedon on several occasions and is believed to have fallen in love with the town. That said, not all of it impressed him.

Of Pissy Corner

> The foul stench I encountered in Clevedon today
> One I found so unfitting for this beautiful town
> Where land meets the channel, such wonder at play
> Till the smell hit me hard, soon bringing me down
> Twas so unexpected, caught me so unaware
> The reek of stale urine did fill the sea air
> The putrid aroma, one I'll never embrace
> I detest Pissy Corner, 'tis a terrible place.

Pissy Corner has been well used for a long time. The problem is that even the highest spring tides never reach it. The smell gets consistently worse over time, especially on hot days and in periods with little rain. Locals have been urged to piss in the sea instead, but this is not always possible for a shivering swimmer who suddenly gets caught short when already dressed after a swim. The use of Pissy Corner, therefore, continued well after Tennyson's visit. It offers a relatively private spot to empty one's bladder, assuming, of course, that nobody is watching from above on the promenade.

Not many realise the part played by Betty and Mildred in the history of Pissy Corner. Betty never set foot on the beach and Mildred only crossed it briefly. However, the decision to allow women to use the beach in the late 19th century would lead to a major conflict over the use of this particular spot of the beach. Women soon objected to the sight of men urinating in the corner of the beach when it became an area for mixed bathing. The men were not happy. One anonymous man wrote to the Clevedon Herald about this.

"The women have only been using our beach for a few months and they are already demanding that we adapt to their needs. I have been pissing in Pissy Corner for years and, before that, my father and grandfather also pissed here. Maybe the women should go back to Ladye Bay if they don't like the way things are done here".

However, the women were not prepared to stand back and allow this unhygienic practice to continue. Hetty Petticoat wrote expressing her disgust in a letter to the Clevedon Times.

"The smell on a hot day is horrendous and makes the beach a most unpleasant place to visit. It's time these men kept their todgers in their pants. If they can't piss in the sea, as God intended, they should hold it in until they get home. Their sordid activities can be viewed by unsuspecting families taking a stroll along the prom. Please make pissing in Pissy Corner a criminal offence immediately".

Mrs. Ethel Gobsworth wrote to the Yatton Yapper. "These men are filthy, disgusting creatures. Part of me regrets the actions of Betty and Mildred. We were happier at Ladye Bay away from the rancid fetor of the pier beach".

After much discussion in local council chambers, a decision was taken in 1893 to build a new public lavatory in Pier Copse, across the road from the beach. A local by-law was passed, prohibiting urination in Pissy Corner. Most people were delighted by this but there were still objectors. A local man, Sidney Trotter, wrote to the Clevedon Times expressing his disappointment.

"The use of Pissy Corner has been a long-held tradition in Clevedon and the new by-law banning its use is extremely disappointing. Whilst I agree that the smells can become extremely unpleasant and unhygienic, perhaps measures could have been taken to ensure that the area was cleaned regularly, rather than banning its use altogether".

Dissenting voices were rare though. The tradition soon came to an end and Pissy Corner was a thing of the past. At least, it seemed that way.

However, an unexpected twist meant that the tradition was revived in the early 21st century. A decision taken by North Somerset Council to charge 20p for use of the public toilets did not go down well. Many were opposed to the plan saying they had already paid their council tax. Others said that they would not always have the necessary spare change on them.

On the 16th of January 2009, a local man, Barry Wigglesworth was arrested for pissing in Pissy Corner. He was ordered to pay a fine of £100 but he refused and the case went to court. Wigglesworth fought the case himself. He argued that, as the toilets were not open 24 hours a day and that he didn't always have a spare 20p on him, it was unreasonable to ban him from using Pissy Corner. The courts found in his favour and the by-law banning pissing at Pissy Corner was cancelled with immediate effect.

Nowadays, you will often see Pissy Corner being used. It is heartwarming to see this historic tradition, dating back to the early 19th century, being revived. Next time you are taking a stroll along the prom, take a look down on the beach and you may be fortunate enough to see a swimmer rushing to Pissy Corner to take a piss having been caught short after their swim.

TWENTY-TWO WAYS

Gertrude tells the story of her longest swim.

"Having completed my first Ladye Bay swim on my twelfth birthday, I would go on to do the same swim hundreds of times over the next fifteen years. My first swim had been a one-way, but I was soon doing two-ways. The one-way swim was only done in the winter months.

I became the first person to complete a Ladye Bay swim in January in 1936. Of course, the friars did the swim all year round, but they got out at the Monks' Steps. I was the first to swim the extra 500 metres. I was extremely proud of my achievement, but I suffered a mild bout of hypothermia afterwards. I would never attempt the swim in January again. Normally, I begin my Ladye Bay season in late March.

In the summer of 1936, I set out on a completely nondescript Ladye Bay two-way with my friend Phillipa. It was a beautiful summer's day and the sea was like glass. It was a neap tide so the current was not especially strong. As we swam under the pier, I turned to Phillipa and told her that I fancied carrying on. I was feeling strong and I fancied seeing how far I could swim against the tide. I turned around to head back for Ladye Bay, thinking I might be able to get as far as the bungalow. I had no expectation of getting any further than that. I just fancied extending my swim a little.

To my knowledge, a four-way Ladye Bay had never even been attempted. I don't think it had even been considered a possibility. Despite this, I was finding progress fairly straightforward. I went past the bungalow and kept going. It didn't take me much longer than normal to reach the hotel. Once there, Ladye Bay is within sight and I saw no reason to not continue. I made it to Ladye Bay without much fuss and then turned to swim back to the pier and complete the first ever four-way Ladye Bay swim. When I arrived back at the beach, I think Phillipa assumed I must have been swimming on the spot for the last 45 minutes. She was quite shocked when I told her I had got as far as Ladye Bay. I was feeling hungry but, otherwise, still felt that I could have carried on if I had wanted to. Phillipa had made a delicious lemon drizzle cake. I enjoyed my slice immensely.

I was delighted to have completed a four-way Ladye Bay swim. With all that excitement, I struggled to sleep that night. I started to think about the possibilities the day's swim had opened up. The swim today had been fairly easy but, surely, it would be much harder to swim against the current mid-tide.

Curiosity got the better of me. The next day, I headed for the beach to swim two and a half hours after high tide. I wanted to see if the swim was possible against the current at its peak. I got in at the slipway and had to work like crazy to get under and past the pier. However, once there, the current became much easier to swim against. The secret seemed to be to stick as close to the rocks as it was safe to do so. The current was much weaker here and swimming up to Ladye Bay was possible, although it took me 45 minutes compared to the usual 20. Now I knew I could do it, my plan was to see how far I could go.

I would set out from the slipway three hours before high tide and see how long I could keep going. I found a day with a very low neap tide and prayed for good weather. Thankfully, I got my wish.

The date was September 17th 1936. I had tried to keep the details of my swim a secret but, somehow, all of Clevedon seemed to know about it. The whole town was buzzing. The beach was packed for my departure and I knew I had a lot of support. I swam with a support boat by my side. They could feed me and keep an eye on my condition. They were in for a long, boring day. Sadly, for me, they weren't the only ones.

What can I say about the swim? I swam up and down, I felt strong and I was well fed. I noticed the crowds getting bigger and bigger the further I swam. Pier beach was packed and the crowds soon filled the beach at Ladye Bay. With the boat beside me and a large orange tow float, I was easy enough to pick out, especially for those with a good vantage point from the coast path.

This was the swim I was most remembered for, even more so than my swim with Her Majesty. It was also the most boring swim of my life.

When I got to sixteen-ways, I made a decision to stop at twenty. I thought that was a nice round number and I doubted that anyone would ever be bored enough to try and beat it. When I got out after twenty lengths, my boat crew told me I had done twenty-two. I fought my way back to the cave through the crowds where, to my surprise, I bumped into Norris McWhirter. He confirmed that I had done twenty-two lengths. I had been so bored on the swim that I lost count. Norris told me that my swim would be included in the next edition of the Guinness Book of Records as the longest ever Ladye Bay swim. I was surprised to learn that he had been there all day. He had kept his presence a secret from me as he didn't want me to feel under any unnecessary pressure.

There were tens of thousands along the sea front by the time I had finished my swim. I could not believe so many had turned out to watch me and cheer me on. The swim was boring but the aftermath made it all worthwhile. Once I was dressed, I was whisked off to the town hall to meet the mayor. It was a great honour. I was starving, though, and could not wait to get away. My first thought was to rush to the Salthouse for a bowl of their wonderful cheesy chips. I then had several more!

A few months later, I was awarded the MBE in the New Years Honours list. My days as a marathon swimmer were over. I had had enough. I would continue to swim but for fun. I had achieved everything I wanted to achieve. With one small exception, which we shall come to a little later".

A SORDID TALE

The decision to allow mixed bathing by the pier meant that Ladye Bay became almost deserted overnight. The beach is a long walk from the main part of the town and very few made the walk or drive up. For years, the beach was a haven of tranquillity apart from the Ladye Bay swimmers who would stop off briefly as they waited for the tide to turn.

Things changed in 1922 when a Mrs. Vera McDowell moved into a house overlooking the bay. Mrs. McDowell was a keen swimmer and loved having the beach more or less to herself. Given the solitude of the place, she felt no need to wear a costume and she began to enjoy the feelings of freedom this created. News of her sordid practices did not stay quiet for long.

A local man, a Mr. Gosslewink, wrote to the Walton Wanderer to express his disapproval.

"I was birdwatching from the viewpoint down by Ladye Bay yesterday when I had the misfortune to observe a local woman bathing at the beach, as naked as the day she was born. I could see everything perfectly through my binoculars. Indeed, I was so shocked by what I saw that I was unable to take my eyes off of her for at least twenty minutes. I was absolutely disgusted by her behaviour and can only hope that the town council puts a stop to these sordid shenanigans".

Unfortunately for Mr. Gosslewink, his letter had the opposite effect to what he had intended. By drawing attention to Mrs. McDowell's tawdry actions, others were encouraged to join her. Mrs. McDowell did not mind the company, in fact, she embraced it. It wasn't long before she had set up a group for Ladye Bay naturists on social media.

Mr. Gosslewink again wrote an angry letter, this time to the Yeo Gazette.

"The beach is now full of naked women. I had the misfortune to take a stroll down there yesterday and I could barely move for all the nudity. The huge crowds had frightened away all birdlife so I had no option but to just sit on the beach and take in the views of the sea and the pier. I felt very uncomfortable".

Birdwatching became increasingly popular at Ladye Bay around this time. The viewpoint would often be full of men with their binoculars. Sadly, for them, there were no birds to see so they all went home disappointed.

The new activities at Ladye Bay posed major problems for the friars on their daily swims. Such holy men could not be subjected to such sordid sights so they were forced to walk down the beach blindfolded. Mrs. McDowell wrote of one such episode in her diary.

"This morning, one of the blindfolded friars tripped and fell on me as he made his way towards the sea. Thankfully, he had a soft landing in my ample bosom and he escaped unhurt. I was then able to guide him towards the water where he was able to swim down to the Monks' Steps and complete his daily penance".

The seedy goings on at Ladye Bay were not in keeping with the standards of a town of Clevedon's social standing. With Ladye Bay so far out of town, a blind eye was turned, but it was certainly never approved of. On hot summer days, there were sometimes as many as fifty naked sunbathers and many hundreds more would look on from the viewpoint or clifftops.

Thankfully, the tradition of naturism at Ladye Bay died out almost overnight. When Francesco's mafia took control of the town in the 1930s, the women were forced to buy swimming costumes and dryrobes against their will. Having paid over the odds for these items, it would have been madness to not wear them.

Mrs. McDowell stood up to the mafia and told them that, as she did not wear a costume on the beach, she would not be buying one. The next morning, she woke up to find that her husband had gone missing. His body washed up on Little Harp beach that evening. Mrs. McDowell was forced to leave Clevedon immediately for her own safety. She died a lonely widow in Burnham-on-Sea in 1958. The days of such sordid activities in Clevedon were gone and, thankfully, they would never return.

SWIM FROM SUICIDE ROCK

Gertrude Higginbottom recalls the time she became the first person to successfully swim form Suicide Rock to the marine lake.

"Most people remember me for my twenty-two-way Ladye Bay swim or for swimming with the Queen. People are surprised when I tell them that, perhaps, my proudest achievement in the waters of Clevedon was my swim from the notorious Suicide Rock. I grew up hearing many stories about this place. It is believed that many had attempted this swim but nobody had been successful. This is the first time I have spoken about it. I did the swim very early on a summer morning when there was nobody around to see what I was up to. If people had known I was attempting the swim they would have probably informed the coastguard and they would have put a stop to the swim before it had begun.

Nobody knows for sure how many have died attempting this swim. Over the years, dozens of bodies have been pulled out from the water between the lake and this notorious spot. It's unknown how many of them had got in the water at Suicide Rock. Some may have been washed downstream after attempting a Ladye Bay swim, but the likelihood is that a large majority were failed Suicide Rockers (or given the name of the place from which they had swum, successful).

Suicide Rock is reached from an overgrown, almost invisible path off of Poet's Walk. The location has inspired much poetry over the years, most notably from Samuel Taylor Coleridge who wrote his famous poem, From Suicide Rock, in 1795.

From Suicide Rock

   Twas a long stumble down through the blackberry and gorse
      Where so many had wandered but so few had returned
      In my folly I was drawn by some biblical force
      With the stories forgotten, so little I'd learned
      Of the dangers inherent in the Suicide Rock
      Looking down from the clifftop at the water below
      I was filled with foreboding and sensations of shock
      At the waves which were married to her sinister flow
      I finally halted, due to fear of a fall
      A view of mortality left me shorn of all grace
      So, I turned back to safety, declining her call
      I would never return to this merciless place.

I remember studying Coleridge's poem at primary school. We had all learnt about the heroism of Betty and Mildred. I wondered what it would be like to be a hero myself- by swimming to the pier from a different direction. Of course, I was too young to even contemplate the swim at that young age but it was something that would always be on my mind.

It was not until I completed my twenty-two Ladye Bay swim that I started to plan for my attempt. I needed a calm sea to give myself the best chance of survival. In the month leading up to my eventual swim, I heard of two deaths which were attributed to failed attempts. I had no desire to join them. I aborted plans for the swim several times when the winds were stronger than I had hoped.

Finally, the day was here. June 28th, 1937. I woke early and set out on my adventure. High tide was at 5.56am which was ideal. There would be little chance of anyone calling the coast guard that early as most people would still be tucked up in bed. My plan was to enter the water no later than 4.30am. This would give me at least an hour and a half to reach the pier. I had no idea how long it would take me to swim around the treacherous headland so I gave myself plenty of leeway.

As I left the safety of Poets' Walk, I was immediately reminded of the words of Coleridge. I had to follow a narrow pathway and my bare legs were scratched by the bramble and gorse which was everywhere. Hardly an ideal start with my legs already bleeding. Eventually, I reached an open space where I was able to look down over Suicide Rock itself. It was absolutely terrifying. The sea was like glass but this didn't stop the waves crashing in against the rock. I have no idea where those waves came from. I considered turning back, as Coleridge had done many years previously, but I was too determined. The climb down was almost vertical. One false step could have seen me fall into the rocky sea below. Any fall would be fatal. Even if I survived the initial fall, I would have shattered many bones and, by the time I was found, it would have been too late.

I gingerly made my way down the cliff face. The last thing I wanted to do was rush but I was well aware that the tide was coming in fast. I needed to give myself plenty of time to get around the headland. I had made a decision to bring my tow float but I soon regretted it as it got in the way and hindered my progress down the cliff. In desperation, I threw it down onto the rocks below. My aim was not as good as it should have been and it was immediately washed away, never to be seen again. Now I was going to have to swim without a tow float. I was terrified.

Eventually, I had negotiated the climb down the cliffs. I was shocked when I passed the dead body of a young man of about my age. I didn't recognise him so he couldn't have been local. I knew he had fallen recently as the tide would have taken his body away otherwise (as it was about to now). At first, I felt a bit sad at the sight of his broken body, blood pouring in all directions., It was not a pleasant one. The initial sadness at this terrible sight passed very quickly when I noticed the jelly babies surrounding his lifeless corpse. I made the most of his loss and helped myself. These would give me the energy I needed to complete the swim.

Having climbed down, I now found myself next to Suicide Rock. I was getting splashed by the waves. It was almost as if the rock itself had magical powers to create these waves in, what was otherwise, a calm sea. The challenge now was to safely enter the sea without being thrown back onto the rocks. I entered the water with trepidation, taking every step very slowly and carefully. I was not going to be rushed. Out of nowhere, a huge wave hit me and knocked me back onto the rocks. Blood was pouring from my arm but nothing seemed broken. Thankfully, I had avoided hitting my head on the rocks which would have, most probably, proved fatal. I had a brief moment of self-doubt and considered giving in but, out of nowhere, another wave appeared, this one taking me straight back out into the water. By a complete miracle, I had been swept away from the rocks and I was (for now), safely in the water. I immediately swam as fast as I could, away from the rocks until I felt confident that I could not be swept back in.

Safe from the perils of Suicide Rock, I was now able to head for the pier. However, I checked the time on my watch and it was already 5.20am, I only had 36 minutes until the tide turned and I still had to get around the headland. The climb down and the perilous entry had taken me a lot longer than I expected. As I swam towards the headland, I could not fail to notice the swirling eddies which were doing everything in their power to halt my progress. I was the first person to swim around that headland. Nobody had ever been there and experienced what conditions the sea had in store. I guessed that sticking close to the shore would make for fiercer eddies. I would not be able to make significant progress and, eventually, I would succumb to hypothermia. After twenty minutes of swimming on the spot, I changed my plan. Instead of swimming under the cliffs towards the lake, I set off for Sand Point which I could just about make out in the distance. If anybody had seen me, they would have wondered what I was up to, but I knew what I was doing. As soon as I had escaped the eddies, I changed direction again and swam back in the direction of the lake.

I was now out in the current and being swept towards my goal. I was flying along but I was in a race with the tide. I could see the pier in the distance but, regrettably, I knew I would not be able to get there. Thankfully, I had time to make it to the lake or I don't know what might have happened to me. I climbed out at the lake, seven minutes after the tide had turned. Much longer and I would not have made it back. You can't swim against the current in the Severn Estuary. I got some funny looks from early morning swimmers as I emerged from the sea and climbed over the wall. I then had to walk back to the pier in my swimming costume to recover my belongings from the cave. I had mixed feelings that day. I knew I had achieved something special but I was not able to share it with anyone. I also knew how close I had come to dying. I was disappointed to have not made it back to the pier but I would not be attempting it a second time. Like Coleridge, I knew that I would never return to that merciless place.

THE WAR AND BEYOND

With the twenty-two-way Ladye Bay swim and an MBE firmly enshrined into her CV, it was time for Gertrude to take a step back. She had been world champion and had become the first person to survive the swim from Suicide Rock. She had achieved all she had wanted as a swimmer. Several weeks before her record-breaking swim, she had got married in a ceremony at St. Andrew's Church. As usual, the whole town had turned out to wish her well.

Gertrude was swimming less and less. It was no surprise when she announced that she was pregnant. Her daughter, Isobel, was born on the 5th of August 1938. Gertrude had plans for a big family. She continued to swim, when she could, at high tide but she no longer had any competitive urges. It seemed that Gertrude would disappear into her family life.

Then, in September 1939, the unthinkable happened. Britain was, again, at war. Gertrude's husband was conscripted to fight in Europe. She would never see him again. Three days after his death, she received a letter from her late husband.

"Dearest Gertrude. It is cold here and we do not have enough food. How I long for the warmth and the comfort of my dryrobe. We are under constant enemy attack and I fear I may never return to you and Isobel. Please remember me in your prayers and pray that God will spare me. I hope, one day soon, we shall be reunited. With all my heart, never forget that I love you both and I shall do for all time".

Gertrude was already heartbroken but she was in complete despair after receiving this letter from the grave. Thankfully, she had the support of her family and she knew she had to remain strong for Isobel. These tragic events inspired her to write this heartbreaking poem.

War

The futility, the pointlessness
The loss of lives so young
Cannon fodder, to those in power
The dead, they lie unsung
Sent to war against their will
Then cut down in their prime
A senseless waste, a bitter pill
Gone well before their time
Reduced to names upon a plaque
Their bodies dumped, deep in the ground
Where once the noise of war was strong
A deathly hush is all around
Mothers, widows, left to grieve
All hope is gone, they can't perceive
The tears, the sweat, the grime and mud
Recalled by medals, soaked in blood
We celebrate this waste of life
We never ask what for
Commemorate futility
And the pointlessness of war.

Clevedon, meanwhile, was believed to be under threat from Nazi bombers. The lake and the pier were both believed to be high on Hitler's hit list. Sadly, Churchill announced the immediate closure of the lake.

"With much regret, my Government and I have decided that Clevedon marine lake should remain closed for the duration of the war. I have spoken to those in control at

MARLENS and the lake is currently being drained. Please do not attempt to swim. The lake has been the scene of much jubilation and celebration over the years, but, we are now facing dark times. This is no time for joviality. The people of Clevedon must concentrate on defeating the Nazis. The lake is a prime target for Hitler's bombers. If we lose this war, we will lose our lake forever. This must not happen".

Sea swimming was banned by the town council soon afterwards. Gertrude had lost the two main loves of her life in close proximity.

Thankfully, England went on to win the war and things, albeit very slowly, started to return to normal. The lake reopened but the popularity of wild swimming did not return to pre-war levels or even come close. The lake was poorly looked after and, slowly but surely, fell into a state of decline.

Gertrude continued swimming in the sea. By this stage, she had been accepted into the swimming club and was allowed access to the bigger cave. Many of the older, more conservative members of the club had passed away since her first sea swim. Dryrobes could now be worn by club members between November 1st and March 31st. Her days as a marathon swimmer were now over but she continued to do Ladye Bay swims.

Gertrude's main focus was on bringing up her daughter, Isobel. Thankfully, she found love and she remarried in 1951. Now approaching 40 years old, her new union would not produce children.

Swimming in Clevedon was now, very much, a minority interest. The Long Swim had been established in 1933 when swimming in Clevedon was at its peak. At this stage, it was a major international event but, post-war, it became a shadow of what it had been. It was restricted to members of the swimming club and few participated. Gertrude always dreamt of winning the Long Swim, but the distance was on the short side for her. She never won it but, remarkably, she finished second on an incredible 19 occasions.

Gertrude didn't stop swimming but the excitement of the 1920s and 1930s seemed a lifetime ago. She was settled into her family life and did not miss her glory days. She remained a massive celebrity in the town, but her fame beyond Clevedon was now almost non-existent. Gertrude was enjoying a quiet life out of the media spotlight and it seemed it would remain that way. However, she would enjoy the occasional day in the spotlight in her later years.

PILGRIMAGE

The friars' daily swims may have become a thing of the past after the second World war but that was not the end of the story.

The friars had originally come over from France and the Church of the Immaculate Conception retained strong links with the Franciscan order across the channel. The friars' daily swim had gained legendary status and Clevedon became a major destination for pilgrimage in the 1950s. French Catholics would visit Clevedon in their thousands during this time. They felt it their duty to do the same swim done by the friars, in order to show penance for their sins. They could be seen in their dozens, sometimes hundreds, walking up to Ladye Bay every day as high tide approached. They would always be wearing their Monks' Trunks, even the women. They would then swim down from Ladye Bay and, hopefully, get out at the Monks' Steps. The steps, though, can be notoriously difficult to find from within the water and it was not uncommon for the pilgrims to miss the steps altogether and end up on the beach by the pier. The locals were not pleased that their normally quiet beach was becoming more and more crowded.

Much worse was the effect that the French visitors had on local cafes. A Mrs. Bertha Mugginsworth wrote to the Tickenham Ticket to express her disapproval.

"I met a friend in Five the Beach today, hoping for a lovely lunch. I was shocked and disgusted to find the menu dominated by garlic, frog's legs and snails. There was nothing to appeal to the locals. We tried Tiffin and Scarlett's and they were just the same. I barely heard an English voice in any of these establishments. My friend and I were forced to venture towards the town centre where we were able to have some proper English food in Jenny's".

Bertha was not the only person to express her disapproval at the new menus. However, the French pilgrims were so numerous that the cafe owners did not care.

Thankfully, Clevedon did not stay a site of pilgrimage for long. The Portishead lifeboat was being called out on an almost daily basis to deal with unprepared and inexperienced French swimmers. The RNLI demanded that the Vatican pay for a new lifeboat, but the Pope refused. Instead, he declared his own disapproval of the swim and demanded that it was stopped immediately. Papal infallibility meant that the pilgrims had no choice but to obey.

The pilgrimages stopped overnight, the cafe menus returned to normal and, once again, Clevedon became a peaceful haven of tranquillity on the North Somerset coast.

ELVIS IN CLEVEDON

When the Clevedon bandstand was refurbished in 1958, it was promised that a big name would be booked to open it. There was much speculation as to whom it may be, but nobody predicted it would be the King of Rock and Roll, Elvis Presley. By 1958, Elvis was already one of the biggest stars in the world. People like Elvis did not come to Clevedon. The majority of Clevedonians were excited by the news. However, a Mr. Patrick Sycamore wrote to the Kingston Seymour Kingdom to express his disgust.

"Clevedon is a backward haven of tranquillity and that is how we would like it to stay. There is no place for this new-fangled rock and roll in our town. I hope others register disgust and let Presley know he is not welcome in our town".

Mrs. Heather Gorse from Weston in Gordano disagreed. She wrote to the South Clevedon Observer to express her support for the King.

"I am no fan of this so-called rock and roll music but we need to move with the times. Clevedon is a very backward-looking town and we need to move forward if we want the town to continue to be a success. I shall not be attending the concert myself but I have purchased tickets for my two daughters. Welcome to Clevedon, Elvis".

Three hundred tickets were put on the market for the concert. Remarkably, they had sold out within a month of being put on sale. Gertrude Higginbottom wrote about the incredible events surrounding the King's visit in her diaries.

"I was 45 years old in 1958 and the new rock and roll thing was not for me. However, my daughter, Isobel, was very excited about the concert and I agreed to accompany her. We got in early and secured two front row tickets. I have to say, I was looking forward to it, despite not being a big fan.

Elvis checked into the Walton Park Hotel the night before the concert. Of course, he was given the best room in the hotel with a magnificent sea view. As high tide approached, Elvis took a look out of the window and was intrigued by the sight of the people swimming past with bright orange floats on their way to Ladye Bay. He called reception and asked what was going on with these swimmers. The receptionist said he was no expert but he knew somebody who was.

I was surprised to receive a call from the hotel. Apparently, Elvis had requested my presence at dinner that night. I said I would attend on the condition that my daughter, Isobel, could attend as well. Elvis agreed to my request and we arrived at the hotel that evening to be met by a wall of Elvis's bodyguards at the entrance to the hotel building. Once they had established our identities, we were allowed in and were led to the dining room where Elvis was waiting for us.

Sadly, for Isobel, there was not much talk of music at the dinner table that evening. The King was clearly fascinated by the swimmers and wanted to know more about them. I told him about Betty and Mildred, my friends Johnny and Freddie, the Ladye Bay swim and, of course, my own exploits. He asked if it would be possible to join me for a swim the next morning. As it happened, the following day was a Wednesday and I would be meeting up in the morning with the Walruses. The Walruses are a group of swimmers who meet at the lake every Wednesday morning. It is often said that anyone who swims on a Wednesday is a Walrus.

Elvis got a very friendly reception the next morning. It soon became clear that he was not a great swimmer but he managed to get to the pontoon and back. He seemed fairly happy with his efforts. Afterwards, Elvis said he would be back to do the Ladye Bay swim one day. We made our way to the Salthouse for lunch and grabbed a couple of tables on Walrus Terrace.

Of course, Elvis opted for a burger, indeed he opted for every burger on the menu (except for the Vegan options which held no interest for him). Elvis was still a young and healthy man at this stage, but his lunch choices hinted at the health problems which would lead to his tragic early demise. Elvis declared the burgers to be amongst the best he had ever tasted. Gary and Andrea were over the moon with his praise and his comments were used in an advertising campaign for the Salthouse for several years afterwards.

Elvis declined the option of a double dip as he had to get back to the hotel to prepare himself for the evenings concert. We all gathered at the bandstand that evening and Elvis performed one hit after another. I loved 'Are You Lonesome Tonight' and 'Return To Sender' but, my favourite was 'Now Or Never' where Elvis had cleverly incorporated the melody from the song from the cornetto ad. I had been converted to an Elvis fan! Everyone went home happy.

We all hoped that Elvis would one day return to Clevedon but, sadly, it was not to be Remarkably, his gig in Clevedon was the only concert he ever performed in Britain. Clevedon remains very proud of this fact and, every year, on the 15th of July (the date of the concert), an Elvis impersonator performs all of his big hits on the bandstand. The event always draws massive crowds

    Clevedon was in mourning in 1977 when Elvis unexpectedly died on the toilet. The flags at the lake were put at half-mast for a week after his death. The town of Clevedon mourned along with the rest of the world".

STIMULATION'S WHAT YOU NEED

One of the proudest moments in Clevedon history came on a cold winter's day in 1977. Gertrude Higginbottom recalls the story.

"There was a real buzz around the town that day. Roy Castle and the Record Breakers team were at the lake and the crowds must have been in the thousands. I remember saying to my husband, I had not seen such massive crowds in the town since my twenty-two-way Ladye Bay swim several decades previously. I don't think many people were expecting to see a world record. We all know what happens to men when they enter ice cold water and we weren't expecting anything different today. I think the main excitement surrounded the presence of Roy Castle and the McWhirter brothers.

I remember seeing Ross McWhirter knelt down on the side of the lake with his thermometer in the water. He confirmed the temperature to be just below freezing and the record attempt was on. A number of regular lake users started arguing with him, saying his readings were incorrect, but McWhirter had top of the range equipment and he wasn't going to listen to them. I believe a few disgruntled lake users went out to buy new thermometers the following day. With overnight temperatures predicted to fall as low as minus twelve centigrade, there was only going to be one opportunity to break the record. The lake was sure to freeze overnight and any further attempts would have to be abandoned.

So it was that Jack McDonald entered the water, proudly wearing his Monks' Trunks. Originally from Scotland, he had recently moved to Clevedon and he was keen to make himself known in his new home town. As he entered the water, Ross McWhirter read out the rules. The use of Viagra was banned, bikini clad women were barred from lakeside (as they could aid arousal) and it was made very clear that nothing below waist height could be shown. Poor Norris had the unenviable task of checking under the water to make sure a state of arousal was achieved. When Norris gave the thumbs up there was a great roar from the crowd. McDonald had become the first man to achieve such a feat underwater in sub-zero temperatures.

To this day, I have no idea how he achieved it. Some refuse to believe he achieved the feat, claiming the McWhirter brothers had been bought off. All the evidence, though, suggests they were beyond reproach and I, for one, believe the record was broken fair and square. Sadly, the film was never shown. BBC bosses deemed the record attempt to be unsuitable for children's TV and demanded that all footage be destroyed. Sadly, only those present were lucky enough to see Roy Castle tap dancing on the side of the lake afterwards to a chorus of "Stimulation, stimulation, stimulation, that's what you need"

Stimulation's What You Need

The Record Breakers team had finally come down
To our lake in little Clevedon, they were welcomed to the town
Our Jack wanted his place in the Guinness book that day
To be the first aroused in sub-zero waters may
Have been a tricky challenge, but he had no plans to fail
When he entered the cold water, he was far too brave to wail
Then Ross announced to one and all that the water was ice cold

And hopes of a world record were alive, our Jack felt bold
Submerged within the water, what he did we'll never know
But it seemed to do the trick and something seemed to grow
A check was necessary so poor Norris grabbed a feel,
At first, he wasn't certain, he thought he'd grabbed an eel
But Jack's arousal soon confirmed, the Clevedon crowd went wild
Jubilation at the lake from every man, woman and child
So, with Jack still excited, he was out of there with speed
Then Roy tap-danced to tell us all- stimulation's what you need.

SWIMMING WITH HER MAJESTY

Gertrude Higginbottom remembers the remarkable occasion when she swam with Her Majesty, Queen Elizabeth II.

"It was the summer of 1979. Her Majesty was visiting Clevedon to open a new branch of B and M and to attend a screening of something or other at the Curzon. Afterwards, she attended lunch in the Sailing Club. Local dignitaries and celebrities were invited including the Mayor of Clevedon and the celebrated bowls player, David Bryant. I was very honoured to also be included on the guestlist, although I did not think myself to be worthy of such esteemed company.

Obviously, I was delighted to meet Her Majesty. Once the small talk was complete, I expected her to move on to the next guest but, to my surprise, she told me she was a lover of open water swimming and she was well aware of my exploits. She told me it was one of her long-held ambitions to complete the pier to Ladye Bay swim and she was wondering if I would accompany her as she thought it unsafe to swim alone. Obviously, I could not refuse such an offer and, after checking tide times on my phone (by sheer luck it was due to be high tide in one hour), we set off on the walk to Ladye Bay.

I remember being very jealous that she was able to walk up to Ladye Bay in her dryrobe. It was a wet and windy day and I would have relished the extra warmth mine provided. There was no way I could have squeezed my dryrobe into my tow float, though, so I had to leave it in the cave and manage without it. Her Majesty was able to hand her dryrobe to one of her butlers when we arrived at Ladye Bay. He was able to run back to the pier beach with it so that it would be there waiting for her on her return.

We entered the water as the tide turned and had a lovely heads-up breaststroke swim as far as the hotel. Obviously, I am unable to reveal full details of our conversation. Her Majesty, though, did speak of her love of open water swimming which she had inherited from her mother. She also spoke of how her mother had told her the story of Betty and Mildred as a child and how it had been her ambition to emulate Mildred's achievement ever since (minus the death bit).

As we passed the hotel, Her Majesty suddenly told me she would race me to the pier. This put me in an awkward position as I could not beat her, but I also didn't want to be seen to patronising her by letting her win. I needn't have worried, as, even swimming flat out, I was unable to keep up with her. She had a wonderful front crawl technique. It was only later I discovered that she was on course to represent Great Britain in the Olympics in 1948 until she picked up a shoulder injury weeks before the games were due to begin.

As we arrived at the beach, I remember the shock on seeing a number of corgis run to the water's edge to greet her. As we all know, dogs are banned from the pier beach, but nobody was going to argue with The Queen. I remember a young faced Gavin Price was in attendance that day. He didn't look happy, but even he wasn't going to tell Her Majesty the corgis weren't welcome.

Once we were dried off and were back in our dryrobes, I was offered a cup of tea. I politely declined as I had not brought a cup. Her Majesty said that wouldn't be a problem as she always had her china tea set with her. To this day, this remains the only time I have had my post swim drink from a cup and saucer. I was also offered cucumber sandwiches (with the crusts cut off) and a slice of Victoria sponge (especially poignant given we were swimming to honour the exploits of Betty and Mildred in Victorian times).

Her Majesty then surprised us all by saying she would love an ice cream. She asked me if there was anywhere nearby where we could get something decent. Of course, I immediately recommended a visit to Aldo's across the road. I have always thought that Her Majesty did not have a big appetite and, with two slices of Victoria sponge inside her, I was expecting her to ask for something small. Even Aldo seemed shocked when Her Majesty asked for an Oyster Delight. I decided to opt for the same (not wishing to offend Her Majesty). As we all know, Her Majesty does not carry cash. She told me that I would have to pay. Of course, I was honoured to do so. Her Majesty finished off her Oyster Delight in a matter of minutes. She said it was the best ice cream she had ever tasted.

Sadly, Her Majesty was unable to hang around as she had to dash off to Yatton to open some orphanage or donkey sanctuary or something. I bade her a fond farewell. That day will live in my memory forever".

Her Majesty's visit made global headlines and made Gertrude world famous. Gertrude had disappeared from the spotlight since the start of World War 2. She did not relish her return to the limelight.

"I live a quiet life these days and I do not wish to be a celebrity. I even had the producers of Strictly Come Dancing on the phone the other day. Of course, I turned them down although I was, for a moment, excited at the prospect of teaming up with Anton Du Beke. I am hoping the press will leave me alone soon, All I want is a peaceful retirement and the chance to spend more time with my daughter Isobel and my new granddaughter, Olivia".

Thankfully, it wasn't long before the media found a new person to hassle and Gertrude got her wish. She went on to enjoy a wonderful retirement, swimming off the pebbles most days and watching her granddaughter grow up. She had lived a wonderful life.

GOODBYE GERTIE

On the morning of the 21st of October, 2002, Gertrude Higginbottom went to the beach for a sea swim. She had celebrated her 90th birthday a few weeks previously. Few could believe she was still swimming in the sea every day. Of course, she was no longer capable of the epic swims of her youth. Gertrude, though, was happy to just get into the water and to have a chat with friends afterwards over a cuppa. In itself, there was nothing remarkable about what happened that morning. Gertrude returned home, where she lived alone having been widowed seven years previously. She wrote about the morning's swim in her diary.

" I had a lovely swim this morning but I am beginning to find it more and more difficult. I am starting to feel my age and I fear I may not have many more swims ahead of me. Part of me feels very sad about this, but what a life swimming has given to me. To still be swimming in the sea daily at my age makes me one of the luckiest people in the world. After my swim, this morning, I wrote a poem, 'To Ladye Bay and Back'. I hope it will be read at my funeral".

Later that day, Gertrude's daughter, Isobel, popped in to check on her mother, as she did every day. Gertrude was sitting in her armchair with a still warm teapot beside her and an unopened packet of Malted Milk biscuits. Isobel could sense immediately that her dear mother had passed on.

As news of her demise spread, the whole town was in a state of shock. The Mayor of Clevedon declared there would be a period of mourning until the funeral had taken place. Her Majesty posted a message of condolence on her social media accounts.

"The swim I had with Gertrude down from Ladye Bay is one of the fondest memories I have of my entire reign. My mother, the Queen Mother, told me the story of Betty and Mildred from a young age and I had long wished to complete the Ladye Bay swim because of it. I will forever be grateful to Gertrude for helping this to happen. Now, when children learn of the Ladye Bay swim in school, they will not just learn about Betty and Mildred, they will also learn about Gertrude Higginbottom. There could be no greater recognition for Gertrude than this. I send my deepest sympathies to Gertrude's family, friends and the town of Clevedon".

Ten days after her death, the day of Gertrude's funeral arrived. A horse drawn carriage made its way from Gertrude's house to St. Andrew's Church, her coffin draped in her dryrobe. Tens of thousands lined the streets of Clevedon to pay their respects. Thousands more could not get into the church for the service. Thankfully, the service was broadcast live on a giant screen on the Salthouse fields so that everybody could partake in a celebration of Gertrude's life. There was not a dry eye anywhere in Clevedon when Isobel read out 'To Ladye Bay and back'.

Gertrude had expressed a wish to be cremated and for her ashes to be scattered in the sea at Ladye Bay, just after high tide. A small gathering of family and friends gathered at Ladye Bay. The ceremony was kept a secret as thousands would have tried to attend if it had been public knowledge.

After a short ceremony, the Dryrobe Song was sung (as requested by Gertrude) and 'To Ladye Bay and Back' was again read out, before her ashes were scattered in the sea.

One final time, Gertrude made her way from Ladye Bay towards the pier, forever reunited with this channel of water which she loved so much.

To Ladye Bay and Back

The swim from Ladye Bay to the pier
A swim I have done many times before
Where Betty and Mildred set out, so brave
Where monks paid their penance on this stormy shore
Departing the bay, pass the hotel up high
Prayers said for Betty, right here, where she fell
Where twenty-two times our Gertie passed by
Then swam with The Queen- through the perilous swell
Where Betty the dog broke records one day
She fought much hostility to show one and all
We can test our limits whenever we swim
Then face our struggles whenever they call
Passing the Monks' Steps, we pause to reflect
On lives long forgotten, of days now long gone
We take it for granted, our freedom to swim
We live for that freedom, the swim carries on
At last, we arrive, swept under the pier
Approaching the beach, the welcome so sweet
We share in the moment, we revel in pride
Now part of her story, our journey complete.

PART TWO

CLEVEDON'S PRESENT

Quentin always brings a packet of Boring Bastards to the lake. Officially known as Malted Milk, unofficially as Cow Biscuits, the Boring Bastards get a very mixed reception. When somebody brings cake, the Boring Bastards stay unopened and unloved. However, desperate times call for desperate measures and, on days when nothing tasty is available, the Boring Bastards come out and most swimmers, albeit reluctantly, help themselves to one. Almost universally, the reaction is one of pleasant surprise that they aren't actually that bad at all.

Hail the Boring Bastards

No milky chocolate topping
No silky custard cream
No ginger, nuts or honey
A long way from my dream

No jam to give some flavour
Exciting they are not
No icing means they're dull and dry
But still, they hit the spot

For Quentin knows when you've had a swim
And you're shivering with cold
They will warm you up, not drag you down
They're a treasure to behold

So, hail the boring bastards
And cherish them with glee
And thank the Lord, if nothing else
At least they're not rich tea.

I first got to know the Swim and Tonics when they were known as the Winter Warriors. The Winter Warriors are a fantastic group run by the wonderful Row Clarke. Introducing new winter swimmers to the joys of cold water, Row gives all the advice needed to keep them safe through a winter of swimming. Amazingly, she offers this service for a mere £5 a time. I was very impressed watching the Warriors from the side of the lake. I get very cold in the lake in the winter months but these brave souls, completely new to winter swimming, didn't seem to get cold at all.

Come the end of winter, their time as Winter Warriors was at an end. They were now fully qualified winter swimmers and they were allowed to leave the nest and swim unsupervised The group had developed a close bond through their winter of swims together. They had become close friends and they were definitely going to continue swimming together. One of them came up with the wonderful name, the Swim and Tonics and their leader, Sarah, designed a Swim and Tonics swimming costume. They even had their own song, to the tune of the Oasis classic, Supersonic.

The Swim and Tonics Song

We love to be ourselves
We can't be no one else
We are the Swim and Tonics, we drink our gin and tonics
When swimming at the lake, we really, really want it
We love to laugh
And take our photographs
Can I swim with you in your wonderful costumes
We can brave the cold and jump in from the pontoon
We eat willy cake
You'll find us Friday mornings at our favourite lake
You need to find a way to swim with us today
We won't swim tomorrow

We're Sarah, Nic, Jean and Aly
Other Nic, Julie, Kate, Sally
And then there's Ruth and her baby
You will always hear us
You will always hear us when we swim
You will always hear us when we swim

We are really loud
We're such a noisy crowd
You'll hear us from the car park
Our screaming is our trademark
We used to be the Warriors but Row no longer wants us
And we really laugh
We take our photographs
We swim when it is freezing, you'll hear us all a-squealing
We're really, really noisy, some people call us crazy

We eat willy cake
You'll find us Friday mornings at our favourite lake

You need to find a way to swim with us today
We won't swim tomorrow

We're Sarah, Nic, Jean and Aly
Other Nic, Julie, Kate Sally
And then there's Ruth and her baby
You will always hear us
You will always hear us when we swim
You will always hear us when we swim.

Me and My Dryrobe

I must admit, I love my dryrobe
And no, it's not a silly phase
Protects me from the ice cold winds
And keeps me warm on wintry days
What better feeling than snug in your dryrobe
When after your swim, whilst sipping tea
Keeps you cosy as you shiver away
Chatting with friends and feeling so free
I feel so special in my dryrobe
I love to wear it all day long
It's great we share a simple uniform
It makes us feel like we belong
They keep us dry, make no mistake
Though wearing them, not always fun
For when the rain starts pissing down
Our dryrobes weigh a f****** ton
Like walking round inside a tent
But, still, they're great for getting changed
We even wear them to the shops
The shoppers think that we're deranged
People say we're all a bit weird
But we don't care what others think
The dryrobe clearly the sexiest look
But they can't be washed and mine's starting to stink
If you don't like the smell then cover your nose
But in my robe, I feel at ease
Call us dryrobe wankers as much as you like
We'll continue to wear them, wherever we please.

I wrote these lyrics to the tune of a well-known carol to commemorate the 2022 Popsicle. The Popsicle is an annual cold-water gala held at Portishead lido, run by the wonderful Emma Pusill. It's one of the highlights of the swimming year.

In The Bleak Midwinter

In the bleak mid-winter
Down in Portishead
Seven-degree water
Filled us all with dread
Early on that morning
Conditions were quite grim
As hordes of crazy people
Turned up for a swim

In the bleak mid-winter
The Popsicle was here
Festive Christmas music
Filled the air with cheer
Then the butterflyers
Got things off to a start
Their bravery inspired us
They really warmed our hearts

The races were aplenty
Crowds cheering from the stands
With hot drinks and with thick gloves
To warm their freezing hands
So many fearless swimmers
Some fast and some were slow

But all of them were heroes
For giving it a go

On to the Grand National
With unicorns to ride
With so much stress and danger
With no safe place to hide
Many jockeys fell off
Into the icy pool
But all would return safely
Unlike the real National

Then the Monday Faffers
Appeared in fancy dress
Obscene and rude as always
But destined for success
With their boobs a sagging
On the frosty ground
The lido full of laughter
They'd surely soon be crowned
But who were these imposters?
A group of tired, old blokes
Hunched over their zimmers
In heavy old man cloaks
They surely were not swimmers
Too old, too frail, too wise
But no, they braved the water
Then ran off with the prize

Before the presentations
A treat it was in store
From those from Almost Synchro
Their synchro was top drawer
So soon the prizes given
Such fun and festive cheer

Come back here next December
We'll see you all next year.

The story of when the Swim and Tonics went for a day out to Studland Bay.

The Return of Naughty Sally Twinkle

The Swim and Tonics went out for the day
To Dorset they ventured, to Studland Bay
With Jean, both Nics and Kate and Aly
Then Julie and Sarah and Ruth and Sally
An early start, they left before dawn
Two cars were filled on that summer morn
For the drive to Studland was a long one for sure
But much fun would be had on this Tonics tour

Two hours had passed before they arrived
With the smell of the sea they soon felt revived
So, they walked to the beach with packed lunches in tow
Plus, their tow floats and whistles, after speaking with Row
They found a nice spot to relax for the day
Away from the hordes so they felt they could play
For the Tonics all knew, they could be rude and loud
And they'd shatter the peace if they stayed with the crowd

Then Sarah stood up, to speak to her troop
I designed these new swimsuits for our wonderful group
But please ensure that you wear them all day
So, we won't lose each other in this beautiful bay
Then Jean made sure to pass on her advice
Stay here on the beach and do not think twice
About wandering off to the other end

There are sights not worth seeing, don't go
there my friends

So, the Tonics relaxed, made the most of the sun
They sunbathed and swam, they were having such
fun
But Sally was curious, she soon slipped away
She wanted to venture to the end of the bay
For Sally was naughty and she couldn't be good
And if somebody told her not to stray, then she
would
So, she walked and she walked on the long, sandy
beach
She was far from the Tonics, she was soon out of
reach

Then what Sally saw, it made her scream
'Twas a man with his todger out, Sally's best
dream!
For the screams weren't of terror, they were
screams full of glee
As Sally dreamt long of being naked and free
In no time at all, Naughty Sally undressed
With the breeze on her skin, she felt calm and blessed
But sadly, for Sally, she was all on her own
All her friends weren't so brave, so she sunbathed
alone

Then panic ensued when the Tonics awoke
From their afternoon naps, it was Just Nic who
spoke
It looks like Sally has disappeared
The group filled with horror, was this what they had
feared?
Other Nic spoke next, we must track Sally down
Before it's too late, she could easily drown

She's forgotten her tow float and her whistle as well
We need to go quickly, there is no time to dwell

I've an idea said Aly, she was next up to talk
Don't forget I swim faster than any Tonic can walk
If I swim down the beach, I'll spot Sally from shore
Then she'll surely be safe and in danger no more
As Aly swam off her friends followed on foot
They knew they must rush, things could soon go kaput
But the Tonics knew not what a shock lay on shore
For they had not a clue of what sights were in store

As they reached the sordid part of the beach
What the Tonics saw would make them screech
I can see the lot screamed Julie in shock
No wonder that Jean warned us not to flock
To this end of the beach, I see willies and bums
Not to mention the boobs, we must leg it my chums
But Ruth made it clear, they could not run away
We need to save Sally from this sordid display

But with so many sunbathers fully exposed
It was hard to find Sally with their eyes fully closed
So, with eyes fully shut, they called out Sally's name
They needed to free her from this cesspit of shame
Then they heard Sally cackle, at last she was found
When they opened their eyes, their jaws dropped to the ground
For Sally just lay there, with the lot on show
And as good as she looked, they could not let that go

Put on your swimsuit, shouted Sarah, so cross
But Sally refused, you are not my boss

But thoughts of concern were consuming Kate
Where on earth is Aly, she seems to be late
So they looked out and saw Aly stuck in the water
Please help her, cried Jean, she's my only daughter
But Aly too shy to swim in to land
With the sight of so many men, naked and tanned

But Sally was brave, to the water she raced
With her bare boobs a-bouncing, after Aly she chased
When she got to her friend, she lay facing the sun
But this was no time to relax or have fun
Like two giant two floats, Aly soon grabbed ahold
Of Sally's bare bosom, was a sight to behold
In no time at all they were safe on the sand
With Aly and Sally both back on dry land

Well, so much relief was filling the air
Sarah said sorry, well it seemed only fair
Thank goodness that Sally didn't listen to me
If she'd worn her swimsuit, Al would still be at sea
My boobs make great floats, beamed Sally with pride
No more swimsuits for me, I have nothing to hide
Then the Tonics all cheered, in that moment 'twas sworn
That they'd all swim as naked as the day they were born.

The Boring Bastards get some horrible abuse but, almost always, they come out on top. This story tells of when the Boring Bastards saved the day after the Walruses cake went missing.

The Boring Bastards Save The Day

The Orcas all gathered for a swim at the beach
They listened intently to Quentin's speech
I've brought along biscuits to eat once we've swum
He was happy to share and so glad they'd all come

So, what sort of biscuits had he brought along?
We all love a biscuit so what could go wrong?
But in no time at all, the smiles turned to sadness
He'd brought Boring Bastards, just what was this madness?

So, Quentin tried hard to pass them around
One after another, they turned the treats down
Lynette had made cake and so had Jo Swim
So the fate of the biscuits was looking quite grim

Even Dave wasn't tempted on that beautiful day
So without any takers, Quentin put them away
Sadly for Quentin, they had been a tough sale
Unloved and unwanted, they were left to go stale

Then Wednesday arrived, a new day would begin
And the biscuits, it seemed, would be chucked in the bin
But with much to be done, they were not thrown away

Running late, Q forgot, it was Walruses day

So, the Walruses met to swim by the pier
The morning was one of such joy and such cheer
They all had a wonderful swim in the sea
Getting out of the water, they were all filled with glee
But a dark, eerie mood was about to descend
Something seems to be missing cried Bev to her friends
Oh no cried out Wendy, I don't have the cake
I brought it to Clevedon but it's down at the lake

They needed to hurry but the lake wasn't far
Most of them walked although some went by car
But when they arrived, the cake was all gone
Were the Sesurlaws guilty? This just wasn't on

Well, the two rival groups nearly came to blows
But the answer wasn't violence as everyone knows
But with no cake to eat and the Walruses weak
There might be one last chance, if they let Quentin speak

Well, there's always my biscuits, but everyone groaned
For the Boring Bastards were already disowned
Quentin was honest, they're not great at first glance
But we have nothing else, so let's give them a chance

So, the Boring Bastards were passed around
And to their surprise, the Walruses found
That they weren't so bad, they had been far too cruel
The Boring Bastards weren't that boring at all.

THE CURSE OF THE BOSSY CAMPER

Tim, Stephen, Jo and Letnet were off on a camping trip to Cornwall. They had found a lovely campsite close to the sea and were all looking forward to a fun swimming holiday. When they arrived at the campsite, it was already early evening. The friends arrived to be welcomed by a stern looking lady. Before they had had a chance to even introduce themselves, the Bossy Camper spoke.

The bossy camper set out the rules
She had so many rules- did she think we were fools?
"For twenty years, we've been coming here
I'll set you straight, don't have any fear
For my knowledge is second to none, you know
I am happy to share the best places to go
I know all the best things to do around here
But you'll do as I say, do I make myself clear?
So, you must obey every rule which I set
If you disobey, I shall never forget
If you break my rules, you'll be hit by a curse
And your trip to Cornwall may well end in a hearse"

Well, the friends didn't know what to make of this woman. To be honest, she sounded a bit crazy. In any case, what were all these rules they were going to have to follow? They didn't have to wait long to find out. The Bossy Camper continued.

"Never dare to visit the Standard pub
The prices too high for the common man
Never swim in the creek, the mud way too deep
In any case, there's a swimming ban

There's a lovely swim out to the pontoon
But never attempt it till well after noon
For the pontoon swim is an evening swim
So have some patience, it will be evening soon
All pasties must be purchased from the General Store
Don't be tempted elsewhere where the price is far more
For a pint, well the Plume is okay, just for one
But only for one, their prices aren't fun
The truth is, you can't beat the Harbour Club
Their prices are fair though they serve no grub
Then when you walk home, at the top of the hill
Don't visit the Standard or you'll lose my goodwill
So, don't you dare stray from my helpful advice
I have spies aplenty and that may not sound nice
But, it's in your best interests to do as I say
So, follow my rules or I'll make you all pay.

Well, on completion of her demands, the Bossy Camper cackled and disappeared into her tent. The friends did not know what to make of her.

"She sounds like a complete fruitcake to me", announced Tim.

"I liked her", said Letnet. "I think we should do as she says. She is only trying to be helpful".

"I can't be bothered to follow her advice", said Stephen.

"Nor me", announced Jo. "We're supposed to be on holiday. Tomorrow I shall break all of her rules".

"I don't think that's wise at all", replied Letnet. "You heard her, she can place a curse on us if we disobey her".

Tim disagreed. "She's a batty old woman. I agree with Jo. Tomorrow we shall break every rule in her poem. When we see that there is no curse, we will be able to enjoy the rest of our holiday".

With that, the friends retired to their tents. They were all excited about whatever adventures tomorrow might bring. They all forgot about the Bossy Camper and went to sleep

The next morning, they woke up, ate their breakfast and got ready to go for a swim. There was no sign of the Bossy Camper. Maybe they had imagined it all. Her tent which had been there the night before had disappeared. Yes, they had imagined it all. There was no need to follow her silly rules.

"Today we shall walk to the local village and swim down to the beach at Towan", announced Jo.

"Sounds like a good plan", replied Letnet. "Let's get going".

So, after much faffing, they were on their way. It took about twenty minutes to reach the village. On their way, they passed The Standard, but it was shut.

"Looks like a nice pub", said Tim. "I think we should pop in there this evening".

"Don't be so stupid Tim", replied Letnet. "You know we've been told not to. In any case, from what the Bossy Camper told us, it sounds far too expensive anyway."

After a short walk down the hill, they arrived at the beach. After much more faffing, they set off on their swim.

Stephen set off first. Unfortunately, he seemed to be heading straight to the pontoon.

"Where on earth is he going?", cried Letnet. "He knows the pontoon is an evening swim".

"Don't be so silly", said Jo. "It looks like fun. I am going to join him".

"Me too", said Tim.

The friends swam in the direction of the pontoon. Letnet reluctantly followed. They climbed the steps up to the pontoon and prepared to jump into the water. Then they heard a familiar voice from the shore and they froze in fear.

"Officer! Officer! There are swimmers on the pontoon. I told them it's an evening swim yet it is still morning. Arrest these people at once. Officer? Officer?"

That was all they heard. They didn't see the Bossy Camper but they recognised her voice

"I told you we should do as she said", whinged Letnet. " Now she has seen us on the pontoon and it's the middle of the morning. She will put a curse on us for sure".

"Don't be silly, Letnet. She's just a silly old lady. Ignore her and enjoy your holiday", replied Jo.

They all jumped off the pontoon and set off on the swim to Towan.

The water was very cold but they soon got used to it. It was a lovely swim along the coast and they arrived at their destination just over an hour later. It was a beautiful beach.

They got out of the water and relaxed for a while, soaking up the sun and warming their bodies which still felt cold from the sea. They were all feeling hungry after their swim.

"I believe there is a cafe a short walk from here", said Stephen. "I've heard they do excellent pasties."

"Well, I hope you won't be buying one" queried Letnet. " You know we've been told to only buy a pasty from the General Stores in the village".

"Sorry Letnet, but I'm starving. I'm not walking all that way just to get a pasty when they sell perfectly good ones here. If you want to go hungry that's up to you".

Tim agreed and he set off with Stephen to find the cafe. When they got there, they ordered one each. A traditional Cornish pasty for Stephen and a vegetable curry one for Tim. They were just about to bite into their pasties when they heard a familiar cry.

"Officer! Officer! These delinquents have just purchased a pasty from the cafe here. I told them to purchase their pasties from the General Stores in the village. Arrest these men at once. Officer? Officer?"

Again, there was no sign of the Bossy Camper, but they recognised that voice. They knew they were being watched and even Tim and Stephen started to feel there may be some truth in her stories.

When Jo and Letnet arrived at the cafe, Tim and Stephen told them what had happened.

"Well, we didn't have one", said Jo. "She is going to come after you two before she comes after me and Letnet".

Of course, Jo was only joshing. She thought it was all a load of nonsense and she was not going to let any of it spoil her holiday.

After lunch they set off on the short walk back to the campsite. Stephen and Jo walked on ahead and it was a very hot day. They both agreed they needed another swim. They saw the footpath down to the creek. Luckily, it was nearly high tide and it would be wonderful for a swim. Jo sent a message to Tim and Letnet so they would know where they were going.

When they got to the creek, it did not look very muddy.

"The Bossy Camper obviously got a bit mixed up", said Stephen. "She obviously meant to not swim in the creek at low tide. It's not muddy at all". Looks perfect for a swim to me.

Eventually, after a long wait, Tim and Letnet arrived.

"What happened to you two?" asked Jo.

" We got lost", said Tim.

"Luckily we bumped into the Bossy Camper and she showed us the way down", said Letnet.

"Oh, for goodness sake", moaned Stephen. "Now she is going to know we are going for a swim in the creek. We will never hear the last of it".

Nevertheless, they all got into the water and swam down the creek. It was very peaceful- until their peace was shattered.

"Officer! Officer! These people are swimming in the creek. I told them not to. It's far too muddy. Arrest these people at once. Officer? Officer?"

Again, there was no sign of the Bossy Camper, but they all knew what they had heard. They swam on down the creek until they reached a little slipway close to the campsite. As they got out of the water, they saw something which turned their blood cold. It was a no swimming sign.

"She was right all along. We should never have been swimming in that creek" said a terrified-sounding Stephen. " We'll be in big trouble if the Harbour Master saw us".

"Nobody saw us", replied Letnet. " Even if they did, so what? The sign says no swimming so we did as they told us and got out of the water".

Stephen seemed to be the only one who was worried about the no swimming sign. They all stood in front of the sign with their swimming costumes on and took photos. Apart from Stephen, they all found it hilarious.

Back at the campsite they were ready for something to eat. Letnet and Jo were ready to cook but Tim said he fancied the pub instead. Letnet and Jo didn't fancy it so they stayed at the campsite whilst Stephen and Tim headed to the village for a few pints and something to eat. The first pub they passed was The Standard.

"We shall have one here" decided Tim. "Then we shall head down to the village and have a few in the Plume".

"What about the curse?", joked Stephen. They both laughed. Neither of them believed a word of that rubbish.

They were glad they decided to visit the Standard. The beer was fantastic and the garden was lovely. The only downside was that Stephen could not get a round in as he was too tall to go inside the pub.

Then, as they sat in the garden, sipping at their beer, it happened again.

"Officer! Officer! These two men are drinking in The Standard when they were clearly told not to. Arrest these men at once. The Standard? The Standard? Officer? Officer?"

Again, there was no sign of the Bossy Camper. Stephen and Tim did not know what to think. They did not believe in curses but they knew what they had heard. A little confused, they set off on the walk down the hill to visit the Plume.

"Now", said Tim. "Remember, we must only have one pint in the Plume before we head to the Harbour Club"

Of course, Tim was joking. They wouldn't be setting foot in the Harbour Club, not with the possibility that the Bossy Camper might be in there.

They downed several pints and had a lovely meal in the Plume. Again, they heard the Officer cries from the Bossy Camper but they were too drunk to care. They walked back to the campsite. On the way, Tim was caught short but, fortunately, he found a nice stile to jump over and there was a nice private spot on the other side where he could empty his bladder. They slept well that night.

The next morning, the whole campsite was awoken by a crescendo of noise emanating from Tim and Stephen's tent.

Song of The Dawn Chorus

Twas not the morning call of the blackbird
Nor the cockerel crow which welcomed the dawn
Nor the nightingale song, one rarely heard
Which forced us awake on that windy morn
The party was long and into the night
They'd dined on sauerkraut and pickled eggs
Downed flagons of beer with all of their might
And out of date pasties discarded by Greggs
The campsite awoke to a wall of sound
From every camper, a tune was composed
From tent-to-tent strong winds did abound
In the breeze the whole campsite seemed exposed
A chorus of joy to warm all their hearts
A song that no symphony ever usurps
Wild celebrations of glorious farts
A hymn to the wonder of the bottom burps.

Well, thanks to Tim and Stephen, Jo and Letnet were up and about early. With the sun up and a lovely day in store, they set off for another swim. The plan was to park up by a pretty church and to walk a couple of miles along the coast path before swimming back. Unfortunately, when they arrived at their destination, the sea seemed to be full of poo.

"Well, we can't swim here", declared Tim. Looks like the water companies have been dumping raw sewage in the sea".

"It's a disgrace" muttered an angry Jo.

"It's the curse", replied Letnet.

They all laughed, apart from Letnet, who was deadly serious.

"We will have to walk back the way we came and find a spot where the sea is less brown", said Tim. "Then we can swim from there back to where we started".

Well, if there was a curse then Tim's quick thinking had saved them from any danger. They had a lovely swim back in clean, clear water. Soon they were back at the car and ready for the lunches which they had prepared earlier. As usual, Stephen was very keen to get eating so he rushed off to search in the churchyard for a picnic table where they would all be able to sit. He found a lovely table, at the edge of a small cliff overlooking the graveyard. Unfortunately for poor Stephen, the table was on a slope and he sat on the lower side. Before he knew it, he was flying through the air.

Near Death in the Graveyard

Stephen searched for a seat for lunch.
"I'll try the churchyard", he said with a hunch
He found a bench but the seats were damp."
But, as we had mats, on our bums we would camp."
We set off to join him, to eat lunch and drink tea.
A tangled heap was all we could see!
"Quick!" called a tourist, "he's had such a fright."
"The bench rolled upon him, I hope he's alright."
We don't know what happened and neither did Steve,
He was trapped by the bench but still able to breathe
Along with the tourist, we grabbed hold of the seat
Untangling legs and his size fourteen feet
Like phoenix from the ashes, our Steve rose again

Alive and intact, and free from all pain.

Tim Clouter 2023.

    The friends had to try and pull Stephen free from the angry bench. The whole tangled mess was in danger of rolling over the cliff. At least Stephen would already be in the graveyard. Thankfully, they managed to stop the bench from carrying Stephen to an unfortunate end. Freed from the bench, Stephen spoke.

    "I never believed it until now but it seems like there is a curse after all".

    "Well, I did warn you", said Letnet smugly.

    Jo and Tim were still having none of it. Indeed, Tim found the whole thing to be hilarious. He regretted the fact that he hadn't taken a photo of Stephen all tangled up in the bench.

    Stephen wasn't enjoying Tim's mickey taking. "I nearly died there. Maybe the curse will hit you next. Let's see if you find that funny".

    "Haha, there's no curse you fool", replied Tim. "Just an unfortunate accident. Anyway, you're completely unhurt so stop whinging. Let's go and get a cup of tea".

    With the curse seemingly lifted, the friends were able to enjoy the rest of the holiday. They had broken every rule which The Bossy Camper had set them and, if there was a curse, Stephen had escaped completely unharmed. The rest of the week flew by as they swam every day and enjoyed the beautiful peace and tranquillity which the area had to offer.

The final day of the holiday arrived too soon. They had a lovely swim and stopped in the village for a cream tea. They were very thirsty after their long swim and Tim, especially, knocked back many cups of tea. They walked back to the campsite feeling a little sad. This was going to be their final evening on this holiday. Tomorrow morning, they would have to pack up and go home.

Of course, all that tea had an effect on Tim. He soon realised he needed to pee. Luckily, he remembered that spot behind the stile where he had peed a few days previously. He ran off on his own, obviously desperate to empty his bladder as he had done without incident a few days before. This time though it was different. The friends heard a cry from behind the stile.

"Help. Help. Call an ambulance. I've broken my ankle. Help".

At first the friends thought he was joking.

Stephen replied,

Oh, silly Timmy, Timmy
Rushing off to have a piss
He climbed the stile and disappeared
Something seemed amiss
Then cries of pain, Tim out of sight
He called for help with all his might
"Help me, help me", poor Timmy cried
"I've broken my ankle, I could have died
All I wanted was to have a pee
I need an ambulance, please rescue me".

The friends soon realised that Tim was not joking.

"It's the curse", said Letnet. " The curse has got Tim".

This time, nobody disagreed with her. They all waited for the ambulance in a terrified silence. Would the curse strike again? If so, who would it strike next? Were they all doomed?

After about half an hour the ambulance arrived. Tim was taken off to hospital.

As the ambulance pulled away with Tim and Jo accompanying him, Stephen and Letnet returned to the campsite.

That evening they heard a familiar, eerie voice.

"Officer! Officer! Hahahahahahaha".

Stephen and Letnet's blood went cold.

THE END.

Little Swimmy Timmy

Little Swimmy Timmy, was walking down a lane;
His bladder was so full, it was causing him some pain.
He nipped over a stile, he needed some relief.
But what happened next, well, it's way beyond belief.
The silly sausage slipped and funked up his poor ankle
His willy stayed within and it didn't get to dangle.
"Quick, call an ambulance" Tim called out to his friends.
They thought that he was joking as they came around the bend.
But joking Timmy wasn't, in agony was he.
So, the friends dialled 999, it was an emergency.
Then Cam came passing by, he was such a lovely fella,
Who sheltered Tim from rain, with his much-needed umbrella.
The others ran back to their tents to get some warm, dry stuff.
While Tim lay in the brambles, his ankle all-a-duff.
The ambulance arrived with two helpful parameds.
They saw Tim's broken ankle and they scratched their worried heads.
Breathe in this gas and air, it will help relieve your pain.
Would have saved a lot of bother if you'd just peed in the lane.
Tim was laying in the mud, the brambles and the clover.
They used a big long board to remove and slide him over.
The ambulance was filthy, Tim had covered it in mud.
But one and all were pleased it wasn't covered in Tim's blood.
The ambulance sped off, rushing Tim to hospital,
With Jo there by his side, there to watch over it all
An x-ray needed urgently, poor Tim was sent away.
His ankle badly broken, twas a sad end to the day
The day had been such fun but it ended in disaster
With Tim laid up in bed, in a dirty, great big plaster.

Tim Clouter 2023

This was written to mark the occasion of Tim Clouter's 65th birthday.

Tim

Have you ever embarked on a Ladye Bay swim
And it's taken so long that the light has grown dim?
Have you turned up at Clevedon to
enjoy the sunrise?
And then stayed there to marvel as the evening sun dies?
Have you dived deep with turtles? Have you conquered the Dart?
Swum the Red Sea with dolphins? Do you have a good heart?
Have you given warm welcomes on those cold winter days?
Have you shared your mulled wine with us waifs and us strays?
Do you love a good photo and a lunch at the pub
In the Salty with friends for their wonderful grub?
Have you double dipped tipsy, after two or three beers?
Have you swum round the pier end without any fears?
If your answer to all of these questions is yes
Then you might be Tim Clouter, at least that's my best guess
If you're Orca and Walrus and Seal all in one
You're most certainly Tim and you re bloody good fun..

This was written to celebrate the 5th anniversary of the Tuesday morning group, the Orcas. The Orcas were founded by the wonderful Claire Paul.

Five Years

Five years of Tuesdays meeting up at the lake
For a morning swim and a well-deserved break
Five years of warm welcomes and the friendships we've grown
With people we otherwise, may never have known
Five years of strange creatures we call token blokes
With their willy warmers and their tired old jokes
Five years warming up on Poets' Walk
With our doggy friends and the chance to talk
Five years of the Salty for a glass of mulled wine
For the chance to reflect and the chance to dine
On a cheesy jacket, or some cheesy chips
Then head back to the lake, for a double dip
Five years of Lugg hugs when we're feeling down
When we're stressed and worried that Kate might drown
Five years of Paul falling off the pontoon
And endless hours pulling off Mad June
Five years of Blodders, with her phone in our face
Five years of joy in our happy place
Five years of cold swims, where we squeal and we scream
Five years where we feel we've been living the dream
Five years of faffing which we hope never ends
Five years of swimming with our wonderful friends
Five years feeling grateful for the fun we all share
So, for five years of Orcas, we say thank you to Claire.

Post swim, especially in winter, we will sometimes go for a stroll around Poets' Walk to warm up. The dogs, which are banned from the lake, will sometimes join us. This is a poem about two of these dogs and their contrasting characters.

Sidney and Senna

Sidney loves Senna and Senna loves Sid
Whilst Senna's the old girl, Sid acts like the kid
Sid never stops running, he sprints way ahead
Only treats entice Senna away from her bed
Poor Sid couldn't manage if Leeza took flight
But Senna won't flinch if her mum leaves her sight
Sidney will hump any dog he can snare
But Senna's too busy, she's washing her hair
These two lovely dogs don't behave as they should
Sidney's too naughty whilst Senna's too good.

My friend, Lindsey Cole, swam from Penarth to Clevedon in a mermaid costume towing a giant poo to raise awareness of how the water companies are dumping sewage in our rivers and seas. This poem was written to thank her for amazing efforts.

The Mermaid and the Poo

The mermaid embraces the allure of the sea
That morning at sunrise, she had set off carefree
From Penarth on to Clevedon was the jaunt for the day
With a wave she was gone, she was off on her way
With a long swim ahead, such a distance to go
Twas made all the more tricky with a big poo to tow
But her spirit was strong, she had nothing to fear
With support of her friends, with her message made clear
For the mermaid was angry at the state of the world
All her stress, all her grief, all her pain was unfurled
In that swim, for raw sewage was destroying the sea
The marine life was dying, this was no way to be
So, to raise some awareness, she'd set off on the swim
As, unless she did something, then the future looked grim
She was well on her way, in her mermaid attire
Came alive in the water, she was off to a flier
Then, she swam and she swam and she swam and she swam
She felt tired and cold but did not give a damn
Many hours had passed but she'd left Wales behind
Now with England so close, saw an end to the grind
Crowds watching from Clevedon saw the boat

closing in
With the mermaid beside, she was going to win!
So they rushed to the slipway, she was out of the sea
And so too, was the poo, all were filled with such glee
But the sewage still flowed, and that wasn't such fun
This was just the beginning, there's still work to be done

Matthew thought that he was being clever when he brought along Boring Bastards with chocolate on. He soon learnt his lesson. The simplicity of the Boring Bastards is what ultimately makes them such a success.

The Chocolate Boring Bastards

As the Orcas gathered for a pre-swim hug
Matthew arrived with a grin, acting smug
Well, you're in for a treat, fellow Orcas, he said
I have Boring Bastards, we will all be well fed

Not Boring Bastards, whinged Andy in despair
Can't we have something nice? It doesn't seem fair
But Matthew explained his treats shouldn't be missed
For the Boring Bastards would come with a twist

Well, I'm starving said Blodders, so whatever it takes
And they can't be worse than Luggers home bakes
So Quentin was told, put your biscuits away
There's no need for your Boring Bastards today

So, what surprise had Matthew in store?
Would there be any need for Q's treats anymore?
Matthew knew that his treats would soon all be gone
For he'd brought Boring Bastards with chocolate on!

Oh my! screamed Brave Karen, well we're in for

a feast
They sound pretty special, or half-decent at least
Claire announced, "first we swim", it was time for some fun
We should all make the most of the morning sun

In the lake, as they swam, for an hour or so
Excitement for the biscuits was beginning to grow
But Q seemed downbeat, he couldn't compete
This time, he knew, he was finally beat

As they finished their swim, it was time to get dressed
Awaiting Matt's treasures, they were all feeling blessed
Matthew called out, who wants one with their tea
All put their hands up, they were all full of glee

For every Orca the answer was yes
But Matthew unwrapped them to find a right mess
The chocolate has melted, you silly fool
You promised us Heaven, this just isn't cool

The biscuits had melted in the morning sun
The dream was over before it had begun
Then Jan said to the group, well, I have an idea
We could eat Quentin's biscuits, I'm sure they're still here

So, Q opened the packet, they were all relieved
And they all felt quite guilty that they hadn't believed
In the plain Boring Bastards, they were finished with speed
They had all learnt their lesson, there was no place for greed.

Professor Wolf

He shivers and shivers and shivers and shivers
He shivers and shivers and shivers and shivers
He shivers and shivers and shivers away
Despite all the shivers he keeps swimming all day
He shivers and shivers and shivers and shivers
He shivers and shivers and shivers and shivers
He only stops swimming for a bite to eat
He swims through the shivers with no thought of defeat
He shivers and shivers and shivers and shivers
He shivers and shivers and shivers and shivers
He shivers and shivers and shivers and shakes
Not a single thought to apply the brakes
A wolf in the water, no chance he could fail
Post swim when he shivers, he looks old and frail
As he shivers and shivers and shivers and shivers
He shivers and shivers and shivers and shivers
And when he emerged from his swim of Loch Ness
My God, he must have been an unholy mess
As he shivered and shivered and shivered and shivered
He shivered and shivered and shivered and shivered
He shivered and shivered and shivered away
But despite all the shivers he keeps swimming all day.

Me and My Cold Hands

I tried to swim this winter
But my hands were far too cold
My friends all said, be braver
But I'm sadly not that bold

My fingers frozen solid
I'm scared I'll lose them all
I've already lost some feeling
Seems I'm heading for a fall

Whenever I'm in water
In the ice, the frost or snow
My feet scream out in agony
But the worst pain, down below

And if my balls should fall off
They will never, ever mend
So I need to be more careful
Or they'll face a brutal end

Each time I get into that lake
My screams, they cause a scene
Perhaps the best solution
Is to buy some neoprene

So, I searched the shops to buy some
But I didn't have much luck
I looked here, there and everywhere
But, found nothing, now I'm stuck

But soon it will be warmer
Now that spring is on the way
And I won't need gloves to take a swim
Once April turns to May.

THE TALE OF STEVIE WEVIE AND HIS COLD HANDS

Stevie Wevie loved to go swimming in Clevedon Marine Lake. He swam there all summer, when the sun was shining and the water was warm. However, it was now winter time and poor Stevie Wevie hated swimming in the winter. Even in the summer, he sometimes found it difficult to get into the water. In winter, he found it was impossible. He would go to the lake and watch all the brave swimmers in the water and he felt very envious. Stevie Wevie had tried to swim in the winter before, but he couldn't cope. The problem for Stevie Wevie was that his hands got very, very cold. Stevie Wevie didn't like getting cold hands.

One Friday morning, in the depths of winter, Stevie Wevie headed for the lake. He always met Luggers and Claire on a Friday and he was very excited about seeing them. He was wearing his dryrobe and had even taken his swimming trunks with him. Stevie Wevie really wanted to swim but he didn't think he would be able to get into the water. He didn't feel brave enough and he was terribly worried about getting cold hands.

The first person Stevie Wevie saw was Gav. Gav was already heading for home on his bike.

"Good morning, Gav", said Stevie Wevie. "Aren't you going to go for a swim?".

"I've been in already", said Gav. "The water is lovely".

Stevie Wevie had his suspicions. Most of the swimmers were shivering away on the side of the lake, but Gav didn't look very cold at all. There was also no sign of a swimming bag on the back of his bike.

"You're very brave Gav", said Stevie Wevie. " I wish I was as brave as you".

"I'm not scared of a bit of cold water", replied Gav. "You should try it yourself one day".

With that, Gav was off on his bike, heading back home for a well-deserved bacon sandwich.

The next people Stevie Wevie bumped into were the Swim and Tonics. Now, the Swim and Tonics were very, very loud. Stevie Wevie could hear them from the Salthouse car park. The Swim and Tonics weren't just loud though. They were also incredibly brave. Stevie Wevie wished he was half as brave as the Swim and Tonics.

"Are you joining us for a swim?" asked Sarah. Sarah was the leader of the Swim and Tonics.

"I'd love to", replied Stevie Wevie, "but, I'm not sure I am brave enough. I'm afraid that I will get cold hands".

"Bless you" replied Just Nic. "We all get cold hands. That's why we wear neoprene gloves. You should get some yourself".

Stevie Wevie wished he could get hold of some neoprene gloves. He had looked in all the shops but he could not find any anywhere.

"I bought mine on the internet", announced Other Nic.

Stevie Wevie had seen some neoprene gloves for sale on the internet but he didn't know what size to buy. In any case, he didn't have a bank account. He didn't see any way of getting hold of some neoprene gloves.

"I can always warm your hands up with my tow floats afterwards", cackled Naughty Sally Twinkle.

Stevie Wevie did not know how to reply to Naughty Sally Twinkle. He would have loved to have had his hands warmed up by her tow floats, but even that offer was not enough to make him brave enough to get into the ice-cold water.

The Swim and Tonics got into the water without a whimper. Stevie Wevie could not believe how brave they were. They all wore neoprene boots and gloves and they all looked as snug as a bunny. Stevie Wevie was very jealous.

The next people Stevie Wevie bumped into were Rita and Jacky. Now, these were two of the bravest people Stevie Wevie knew. They were so brave that they had even swum in the Arctic Circle. Stevie Wevie wondered how cold his hands would get if he ever swam in the Arctic Circle, but he knew that he would never find out. He was nowhere near brave enough to try it. Rita and Jacky were so brave that they swam all the way to the end of the lake and all the way back again. Stevie Wevie could not believe that they swam all the way around the lake, even in the depths of winter.

"Are you going to join us for a couple of laps?" asked Rita. "We are only going to do two today as the water is very, very cold".

"I'm afraid I won't be able to join you today as I am not brave enough", replied Stevie Wevie. "I am worried I will get cold hands and my fingers might fall off. I hope you both have a lovely swim".

Stevie Wevie looked on with envy as the brave ladies got in the water without any screams and immediately put their heads down for two laps of front crawl.

The next person Stevie Wevie saw was Brave Karen. Now, Brave Karen was incredibly brave. Everybody said that Brave Karen was as brave as brave can be. Stevie Wevie had a question for Brave Karen.

"Good morning Brave Karen", said Stevie Wevie.

"Good morning, Stevie Wevie" said Brave Karen.

"Brave Karen, everybody knows that you are incredibly brave", started Stevie Wevie. " I would love to be as brave as you one day. I've been wondering, do you get a cold head when you go swimming in the winter?".

"I never get a cold head", replied Brave Karen. "Not only do I have neoprene gloves and boots but I also have a neoprene hat".

Stevie Wevie was very impressed. He watched as Brave Karen put on her neoprene gloves, her neoprene boots and her neoprene hat.

"Are you going to join me for a swim?" asked Brave Karen.

"Not today", replied Stevie Wevie. "The water is far too cold for me and I am afraid that I am not brave enough. Have a good swim".

With that, Brave Karen was off. She got into the water without any fuss and set off to swim to the end of the lake. He could see how she had earned her nickname. She was, indeed, very, very brave.

The next person Stevie Wevie saw was Professor Wolf. Professor Wolf was wearing his dryrobe and he looked like he had already swum. Unlike Gav, earlier, he looked very cold and he was shivering and shivering away. Professor Wolf was incredibly brave. He didn't wear neoprene gloves and he certainly didn't have a neoprene hat. Stevie Wevie looked at Professor Wolf very enviously. He wished that he was as brave as Professor Wolf. Professor Wolf was so brave that he had been swimming in Loch Ness with the Loch Ness monster. However, this was not the bravest thing Professor Wolf had ever done. The bravest thing Professor Wolf had ever done was swim in the lake in winter without any neoprene gloves

"How far have you swum today?" asked Stevie Wevie.

"Just six lengths today" replied Professor Wolf. "The water is very, very cold so I thought that was plenty".

Stevie Wevie was very jealous. He could swim six lengths in the summer but, in the winter? Not a chance. Stevie Wevie wished he could swim six metres in the winter but he couldn't even manage that. Stevie Wevie wished Professor Wolf well as he continued to shiver away.

The next people Stevie Wevie saw were Bendy Wendy and Tumble Tebay.

"Good morning, Stevie Wevie", said Bendy Wendy and Tumble Tebay. "Are you going to join us for a swim?".

"I'm afraid not" answered Stevie Wevie. "The water is far too cold for me and I am scared of getting cold hands"

"That's a shame", said Bendy Wendy. "We're going to swim to the pontoon".

"Then we're going to do backflips into the water", announced Tumble Tebay.

Stevie Wevie could not believe how brave they were. He was too frightened to even get into the water. He would never be brave enough to jump in from the pontoon in the depths of winter.

Stevie Wevie watched on enviously as Bendy Wendy and Tumble Tebay backflipped into the lake from the pontoon. Tumble Tebay's effort was much better than Bendy Wendy's but that wasn't important. The important thing was that Bendy Wendy had been brave enough to attempt it in the first place.

Stevie Wevie was beginning to feel fed up. He really wanted to swim in the lake. If only he could be as brave as everyone else. He was just about to give up when Claire and Luggers (finally) turned up. Stevie Wevie was delighted to see Claire and Luggers. Most of all, he was excited about receiving a Lugg hug. He was feeling very down due to his lack of bravery and he knew that a Lugg hug would cheer him up. Luggers gave the best hugs in the world. After the Lugg hug, Claire and Luggers asked Stevie Wevie if he had been in the water yet.

"I'm afraid not", replied Stevie Wevie. The water's way too cold for me and I am sadly not that brave. My hands get very cold and I am scared that my fingers may fall off. I have been watching everyone else be brave and I feel like a wimp.

"There's no need to feel like that", replied Luggers. "It doesn't matter if you are brave or not. The important thing is that you are a good person. God loves everyone equally, even people who get cold hands".

Everybody gathered around Stevie Wevie. Well, everyone apart from Gav. He was still at home eating his bacon sandwich. Stevie Wevie did not know what was going on.

Then, Claire spoke.

"We have a surprise for you Stevie Wevie. We all clubbed together and we bought you a present"

Stevie Wevie was overwhelmed and he was very thankful that his friends had bought him a present. He didn't feel as if he deserved it though. They were all far braver than him. As Stevie Wevie unwrapped the present, he felt glad that he had not been brave enough to go for a swim. If he had, his hands would now be very, very cold indeed and he would not be able to open his gift.

"We've bought you something to help you swim", said Claire. "Everyone pitched in".

When Stevie Wevie finished unwrapping his present, he could not believe his eyes. It was a pair of neoprene gloves! Exactly what he had been hoping for. Stevie Wevie had a tear in his eye. He could not believe how thoughtful and kind his friends had been.

"Thank you everybody", said Stevie Wevie. "Now, let's get in the water and try these bad boys out!",

Everyone got into the lake and joined Stevie Wevie for a swim to the pontoon. Stevie Wevie felt very brave and his hands did not feel cold at all. He swam all the way around the pontoon and back to the steps. His hands were super snug and his fingers did not fall off.

The friends got out of the lake and, once they were dressed, they celebrated with a glass of mulled wine. Everyone felt snug and warm in their dryrobes and the mulled wine warmed them up even more. Stevie Wevie was so grateful. His swimming friends were the best friends in the whole world.

Song of the Mermaids

The Song of the Mermaids
Where a kinship is shared
Where my swim sisters swim
Where my soul is repaired
Where the water refreshes
Where no boundaries are crossed
With the mermaids beside me
I no longer feel lost
In the chill of the ocean
Where their problems are faced
Where talking is everything
Where their truth is embraced
Theirs the song of the sea
Whether mother or daughter
Where their souls are transformed
By the cold, healing water
As a man in their midst
I am freed from life's storm
Patriarchy abandoned
And, their welcome, so warm
Where my faith is replenished
Where my mood is in tune
With the roar of the sea
With the glare of the moon
Where the sea angels found me
I still find them today
Mother Nature my saviour
Watch the mermaids at play
In the cruel, icy water
They are stronger than me
Here, the Song of the Mermaids
Fills the depths of the sea.

EPILOGUE

In the 1960s, Clevedon was struggling to compete with local rival Weston-Super-Mare. The Clevedon tourist board held a poetry competition to find a poem which would best promote Clevedon over its local rival. Gertrude Higginbottom was best known for her swimming exploits, but she was also known to write the occasional poem. She entered the competition and she won.

The Weston-Super-Mare tourist board were not happy with the poem. They took their Clevedon counterparts to court to prevent the poem from being published. Their argument was that the poem contained a number of falsehoods. At the time, the public toilets in Weston were free to use (decimalised money had not even been introduced when the poem was written) and the Tropicana and Birnbeck Pier were still in perfect condition. Sadly, the courts sided with Weston and the poem was never published. An inferior poem was used instead and Clevedon went into a terminal decline as a tourism hotspot, not helped by the collapse of the pier, shortly afterwards.

I recently came across the poem whilst searching through Gertrude's diaries. Remarkably, everything she spoke of in the poem was to come true. The poem could have been written in 2023. Indeed, it is almost as if I made the whole thing up.

Anyway, for the first time ever, here is Gertrude's long-lost poem.

Visit Clevedon

I've heard a lot of people
Put down Weston-Super-Mare
Some say they're being cruel,
But I think they're being fair
The dilapidated buildings
Decay is all around
The pier is truly awful
It isn't worth your pound
The marine lake is substandard,
Full of mud with no pontoon
The Tropicana and Birnbeck Pier
Look ready to fall down soon
So instead, come visit Clevedon
It's a much more pleasant town
There's less mud and the pier superior
She will never let you down
Okay, she's lacking candy floss
And the stench of stale hot dogs
And although both towns charge 20p
Clevedon has much nicer bogs
So next time visit Clevedon
You can park your car for free
Instead of dirty Weston,
I am certain you'll agree.

I WISH I WERE A MERMAID

I wish I were a mermaid
Forever in the sea
A life of peace and solitude
My days spent worry free
No need to stress; 'bout trivia
No time for harsh regret
Untroubled in the water
The chance to soon forget
Adversity and tragedy
Submerged I'm full of glee
So, here's to all the mermaids
Forever in the sea.

Gertrude Higginbottom 1932.

Printed in Great Britain
by Amazon